ERIC GOEBELBECKER

MURDER IN SOFT WORDS

THE GREAT WAR OF THE WORLDS BOOK #3

Trick of the Tale LLC

25 Veterans Plaza #5279

Bergenfield, NJ 07621-9998

Trick of the Tale

For Amy, who makes me want to be a better author.

FOREWORD

The Great War of the Worlds stories are set in a universe where H.G. Wells's War of the Worlds happened.

In 1894, aliens crashed to Earth in spacecraft that operated like meteorites. They attacked us with fearsome weapons like Black Smoke, a chemical weapon and heat rays that can melt steel in a few seconds. Then, they built processing centers and used humans for food.

But the attack ended quickly because the Martians, if that was where they really came from, weren't prepared to deal with Earth's microbes and died from disease.

What happened after the attack? What did humanity do with the technology the Martians left behind?

"Nothing is hopeless that is right."
- Susan B. Anthony

CHAPTER 1

Susan picked up the newspaper, tucked it under her arm, and reached into her purse for the key to the Edison radio team's office. But before she opened the door to start the workday, she took a moment for herself.

Leaves rustling in a light wind provided the ideal background for the chatter and twitter of birds and a particularly angry squirrel. Together, they created the perfect accompaniment for a cool Wednesday morning in late September. The perfect start to a day for some early apple picking or sitting on the front porch with a book and a warm drink. Not a day for working in a stuffy office, with needy engineers and a cantankerous army officer.

When was the last time Susan had enjoyed the weather? When was the last time she had taken a day off to relax? Six months ago? Seven? Longer than that. The year 1915 was three-quarters over, and it had been a whirlwind.

It had all started on New Year's Eve, when James, Susan's fiancé, had been called to Long Island to fix the radios that the United States used to talk to Europe and the Planetary Warning System. When he'd arrived, he'd uncovered evidence of interference. It became the start of a trail that had led him, Susan, and a marine named Reynolds, to a conspiracy to conceal the return of the Martians.

Susan shook her head to clear away the memories of conspiracies and violence, balanced the newspaper on the box of Danish from Verps Bakery on her left hand, and unlocked the door with her right. Then she headed to the break room to start coffee. She'd already had a cup before leaving home, but General Ross would be in soon; and neither James nor Stephen Seward, the radio team's remaining senior engineer, would remember to start the percolator on their own. It was up to her to make sure the general received the attention he wanted.

But Susan would need to do more than just lay out the pastries and start the coffee, as she discovered. Piles of breadcrumbs adorned each end of the break room table, an array of napkins was scattered across the floor, and a collection of dirty dishes cluttered the sink. James and Seward must have worked late enough on the transmitters for the National Radio Network that the mess was made after the cleaning crew had gone home. Susan had discussed with James whether the crew could come later, but James hadn't done anything about it yet. Susan would have to make the call herself now, after cleaning up this shambles of a break room first.

Of course, she knew General Ross well enough to guess what he would say about the transmitters, which were due to be tested in just a few weeks. They were already overdue and the engineers had been working late in an effort to avoid his wrath.

Susan put down the Danish, removed the lid from the coffeepot, and placed it on the counter before reaching in to remove the filter basket full of last night's grounds. But she hadn't noticed the shaker that one of the engineers must have left on the counter. She brushed it with her elbow, scattering salt across the maple countertop and onto the floor.

"Bad luck!" Mom would have said, only half kidding.

Susan had lost both of her parents in the first Martian Attack. She'd been in school the morning the aliens had arrived in

Ridgewood with their terrifying walking machines. They'd taken thirty-five people from the area around the train station and opera house, somehow missing the Beech Street School a few streets away. Good luck for Susan and the rest of the village kids. Not for Mom and Dad.

Susan brushed a tear from one eye and started the coffee. As she finished wiping up the unlucky salt, a clatter echoed from outside the break room. Who was in the office already? Why had they locked the door after coming inside? Had James never gone home? He'd slept on a lab bench before. Was he really so worried about finishing the transmitters for General Ross?

"Is someone there?" she said as she left the break room and headed toward the labs. Brisk footsteps echoed off the cinder block walls, but the long hallway that led to the loading dock at the back of the building was empty.

Susan stepped into the smaller workshop where Seward and James had been laboring yesterday. Components littered the workbenches on either side of the room, but there was no sign of either engineer. The doorway to the larger workshop was partly blocked by a wooden crate about the size of a steamer trunk. It rested on the floor directly in front of the door, as if whoever had wheeled it in on a hand truck and gotten out fast. Was that what Susan had heard through the wall they shared? She checked the hall again. No one was there.

That crate couldn't stay there. What if General Ross saw it? What would he think? Susan started down the loading dock, then caught herself. She had work to do first. She'd deal with this mess after she cleaned up the wreckage from last night and completed her morning rounds.

She went back to the break room, finished tidying up, picked up the newspaper, and walked down the narrow hall to Ben Johnson's office—No. It was James Brogan's office now. Susan still hadn't adjusted to Ben's disappearance during the chaos earlier in the year.

She left the paper on James's desk, catching a glimpse of the photograph of Ben Johnson standing next to Thomas Edison that hung behind it. It had been Ben who had hired her as a clerk, allowed her to expand her responsibilities, and even introduced her to James.

What had happened to Ben? Was he really dead?

Susan finally made it to her desk. She shared an office with Noah Abrams, the radio team's head of supply. Noah had been putting in some long hours, too, working with General Electric on getting the radios built, tested, and distributed for the pilot program.

A new report from late yesterday was still on Susan's desk. It contained transcripts from the latest transmissions from Europe, including an interesting report from the Planetary Warning station in Paris. The men who had led the fight against the Martians in Reims had set up shop in the French capital and wanted to speak to James again. Susan was still underlining the relevant parts of the report when a shout broke her concentration.

"Where the hell is everyone?"

Wonderful. General Ross had come in early. And James was probably still dead asleep at home. Susan reached for her desk phone. She could at least ask his mother to rouse him out of bed.

"Does anyone in this office work for a living?" the general bellowed, his voice echoing from down the hall.

Susan knew it wouldn't do to be caught on the phone with the team leader's mother when the general barged into her office. She put the phone down and stepped into the hallway. "General Ross!" she said, forcing a bright smile. "You're here bright and early."

"Where's Brogan?" the general growled. "Where are my transmitters?" His driver, a young man in a neatly pressed uniform with silver insignia marking him as either a captain or a lieutenant, was hanging back near the entrance to the break room.

"I'm sure Mr. Brogan will be here soon, General," Susan said.

"He was working on the systems late last night. Can I get you some coffee and a Danish?" She edged past the general, gently excusing herself to his driver, and into the break room, hoping fresh coffee and a pastry would change the subject. She was already pouring his cup when the general followed her into the room.

"I need those transmitters now," the general said as he dropped his bulk into a chair and waited for service. "Does Brogan understand how tenuous his position is? I've got plenty of radio techs in the War Department who would kill to take over this project. They'd even show up for work in the morning."

Was the general serious? Or were his threats just more of his typical bluster? James had been the logical choice to take over the team after Ben Johnson's disappearance. He understood the technology better than anyone else. He had worked shoulder to shoulder with Ben for years, and no one—not even Seward—understood it as well as James did.

But the best engineer wasn't always the best choice for manager. And that might have been the case with James. He spent too much time focused on details and not enough on overseeing the entire operation.

General Ross propped his elbows on the table. His bulky gray mustache twitched as he raised a finger—a sure sign that he was about to launch into a tirade.

"I'm sure the transmitters are nearly ready, sir," Susan interjected. She had to serve the old grouch, but she didn't have to endure his jeremiads. Once she placed a mug of coffee in front of him, she asked, "Cheese Danish? Or cherry?"

"No crumb cake this time?" the general asked.

There was—and he would have known that if he had gotten up and checked the box for himself. Susan had been hoping to save it for herself, but she put the crumb cake on a plate and brought it to General Ross.

"Thank you," he grumbled.

"You're welcome," Susan said as she walked back to the coffeepot to pour a cup for the driver. She turned to ask him how he took it—

A deafening roar drowned out her request. Susan was swept off her feet and thrown out the door into the office hallway.

The hallway, and then the world, went black.

Susan woke up in the hallway with the taste of blood in her mouth. A sharp pain in her left side made her yelp as she struggled to her feet. But did she yelp? She couldn't tell because she couldn't hear anything just then.

What happened? She fought back nausea and limped into the break room.

The large workshop was visible past the pile of plaster and lathe that used to be the far wall of the break room. Large, jagged splinters littered the floor of the work area and tugged at Susan's fuzzy memory.

The crate. The splinters were from the mysterious crate that had partly blocked the doorway into the workshop.

General Ross was lying on the floor near the break room doorway. He started to sit up but fell back onto his back. His mouth moved, but Susan couldn't hear him.

"General!" Susan said, the pain in her side flaring. "Are you okay?"

She scanned the room, looking for the general's driver. A single boot protruded from the pile of rubble that used to be a wall.

CHAPTER 2

Susan shuffled down Nassau Street, thanks to the pain from the bruise forming on her left side. She had no reason to rush, either. James was bound to be late, even for their first meal together since the attack at Edison.

Attack.

That was what General Ross had called it when—against his doctor's orders—he'd stolen from his hospital room to Susan's the morning after the explosion. She'd only suffered a few scrapes and bruises from flying debris, while the general had six stitches on the right side of his head. His driver, however, was still in a coma.

Susan checked her watch as she reached the Inn. It wasn't eleven thirty yet. Why had James insisted on lunch here? There was no way he'd get out of the office on time, especially on the first day after the office reopened.

She ignored the tightness around her ribs and kept walking. At least the ringing in her ears had subsided, so she could have a reasonable conversation with James when they met. It was too pleasant outside to spend an extra half hour sitting at a restaurant table. Or more than a half hour, if she was right about James. He'd be busy assessing the impact the explosion would have on the National Radio Network. To Susan, the word *explosion* sounded better than *attack,* if for no other reason than it let her off the hook for not raising an alarm about that crate. If she had, the general's driver would be awake and listening to his boss complain about traffic, instead of wasting away in a hospital bed.

Her side ached as she reached Renwick's, so she stopped and leaned against a lamppost. Perhaps walking here from her room at Mrs. Prendick's had been too ambitious, but the idea of calling a cab had seemed extravagant.

"Susan?" asked a voice from behind her. "Should you be up and about already?"

Susan spun around in surprise—which didn't help the pain in her side—to see the rumpled form of Carl Urich.

"Mr. Urich!" Susan said. "You're in West Orange today? Are you following a story? Or visiting your favorite lunch spot?"

"A little of both," he replied. "I heard your office reopened today, and since no one will take my calls, I'm going over there to talk to James in person. I didn't expect to see you at all. I thought you'd still be recuperating." Carl was a reporter from *The Spectator*, a newspaper out of New York City. He'd been instrumental in helping Susan and James uncover the conspiracy to disable the transatlantic radios in Sayville last year. The linen blazer he was wearing clashed with not only his pants, but everything in New Jersey.

"I'm hoping to head back to work tomorrow . . . or Wednesday," Susan said, wondering how ridiculous that sounded as she leaned against a lamppost and hugged herself in pain.

"I'm sure they need you, but they'd want you to make it back in one piece. Here." Carl extended an arm and gestured toward the outdoor tables at Renwick's. "Why don't you let me help you take a seat?"

Susan took his arm and let him guide her to a table. It felt as if the ground shifted under her as she lowered herself into a chair.

"Are you okay, Susan?" Carl asked, sounding genuinely concerned. "You look a little gray."

"I'm fine, Mr. Urich. A little bruised, but at least my hearing has recovered." As she spoke, Susan thought about how much worse the driver and the general had fared in the explosion.

"Call me Carl, please. We've known each other for months. I was concerned when I heard about the attack." He gestured toward the restaurant window for service, then sat across from Susan.

Attack. There was that word again.

"Since you already know that the office is reopening today, do you have an idea of why the Black Army targeted us?" Susan asked.

"To be honest, I don't think it was them," Carl said.

Susan leaned back in surprise. The Black Army was a group of anarchists fighting what they—and many others—called the Bryan administration's "tyranny." They'd attacked theaters, train stations, and even the Hudson Tubes, disabling the trains for a week in February. She has immediately assumed they were responsible for the bomb. Who else could it be?

"Attacks like this have become a part of life over in the city," Carl continued, "and it's natural to assume that it was the Black Army. It's also convenient for the government to blame everything on them. But they've been going for high-profile, public places. They're more interested in attracting attention than executing on strategy. This wasn't the first time we've seen an attack on something more strategic than a train station or public square. But it was the first one in New Jersey, and it's shocking to see Edison has become a target."

Susan knew that no one would ever accuse Carl Urich of accepting the government's claims at face value. But the Black Army had been responsible for numerous bombings around New York, Chicago, and all the way over in San Francisco. Why wouldn't they be the primary suspects for this explosion?

"Hello, Mr. Urich!" said Penny, the regular waitress at 'Wicks. "And you too, Susan."

"Good morning, Penny," Carl answered. "I'd like the usual, and I'll take care of whatever Susan is having."

"Nothing for me today, thanks . . . uh, Carl," Susan said. "I'm meeting James for lunch at the Inn." She waited until Penny had stepped away before continuing. "So you think it's someone else? A different group? Every story I've seen said it was them. Even the Security Police who spoke to me seemed to think so." As soon as Penny was out of earshot, she whispered, "Have you heard something else from them?"

The Security Police always kept a tight lid on stories like this one, especially since earlier in the year, when Sean Fleming, one of their own, had gone rogue inside Edison. Susan wouldn't have been surprised if they'd suppressed all word of the explosion, but the story had appeared in all the local papers.

"No, I haven't," said Carl with a grimace. "But it's always easier to fall back on a comfortable lie than look for the difficult truth. I was working on a story about some disappearances in Manhattan, but when I heard about the explosion, I thought it might point to a bigger story."

"Bigger than me almost getting killed?" Susan asked with a wry smile.

"That's the story they won't let me print. It would mean panic in the streets." He grinned back. "I'm glad to see you can laugh about this. It's the best defense."

"They say it's the best medicine."

Carl smiled again, but his expression shifted for a moment, implying he'd been on the receiving end of an attack at least once. Susan sighed as the throbbing in her side lessened.

"Are you sure you're okay?" Carl asked.

"Yeah. I overdid it a bit getting over here."

Penny arrived with Carl's coffee. "I'll be right back with your breakfast, sir," she said as she deftly placed the mug in front of him, along with a tiny pitcher of cream and a bowl of sugar cubes.

"When is your lunch?" Carl asked Susan.

"Noon," she said, checking her watch again. Eleven forty-five. Plenty of time to rest her side.

"The National Radio Network is hardly a secret," Carl said as he dropped three cubes of sugar into his coffee. "The Bryan administration distracted everyone from a conspiracy inside the SPs by announcing it. And once it's up and running, they won't need to coerce the press to spread their lies."

"That's a little cynical. A public radio network could save a lot of lives."

"It certainly could," Carl said as he stirred his coffee. "It could also be a tool for bypassing a free press. Now, let's say someone feels even more strongly about Bryan's public network. Let's say they want to stop it. Wouldn't destroying the prototype transmitters be a good start?"

The ground shifted under Susan again, but not because of the pain in her side. A few months ago, the radios Edison maintained on Long Island had been a target. Now her office was?

"I knew the transmitters were being built here, because I have friends in the area. But it's not public knowledge. So who else was aware of what your team was building here? Do you have any ideas?" Carl raised an eyebrow as he asked the question.

"General Electric is making the prototype receivers for distribution to strategic locations, and Edison is building the first pair of transmitters," Susan said. "That's not a secret, is it?"

Where was Carl going with this? Was he saying that someone inside Edison had planted that bomb? Or was working with whoever had? And just like that, Susan was aware she had gone from a friend recovering from an attack to a source for Carl's next story.

"Who's building the radio equipment isn't a secret, but where and how is," Carl said. "I haven't started to think about how GE is going to produce enough receivers to make this system scale. But that's not the story—at least not yet. Plenty of people have reasons to oppose this project, so basic operational security makes sense. How did the attackers know where to plant that bomb?"

Susan's throat went dry. She wished she had accepted Carl's offer for at least a cup of coffee. For the second time in less than a year, she was being plunged into games of deceit and death. She had worked hard to expand her responsibilities beyond typing and filing at Edison, but rooting out spies wasn't a job she was interested in. Even though she'd helped James do it once already.

She looked down at the table before answering. "I don't know, Mr. Ur—I mean, Carl."

Carl smiled. "I'm sorry. You're still recovering. You don't need the third degree from me."

Just then, Penny arrived with a plate of eggs and toast.

"I should let you eat, and get to my lunch," Susan said.

"Sure thing. You can tell James I'll be checking in on him later. I'm sure he'll appreciate the warning." Carl laughed then.

Susan stood and started back down the street toward the Inn, happy to leave behind Carl Urich's questions about the attack at Edison. In her opinion, it was up to the press and the Security Police to root out spies.

Not her.

CHAPTER 3

As Susan looked up from checking her watch one more time, she nearly stumbled. James was already seated at their customary table at the Inn. He was at least three minutes early.

"You made it!" she said, suppressing a wince as she slid into her chair.

"There's only a few of us in the office, and the general won't make it today," James said.

"That's good. How bad is the kitchen? Did the explosion damage the transmitters, too? Hopefully, you can get a lot of the cleanup done before the general tries to take charge." Focusing on the details of getting things back to normal at Edison, rather than rooting out another spy, was comforting for Susan.

"The general means well. At least his motivations are in the right place." James was always one to look for the best in people, even to his own detriment. He was quick to defend General Ross, though his boss rarely had a positive word to say about him. To Susan, that was one of James's most endearing qualities.

"Well, I think I can start helping out tomorrow," Susan said, smiling again.

"So soon?" James said, looking genuinely concerned. "Are

you sure you're ready? I'd understand if you never wanted to go there again."

"That's sweet of you. But of course I want to go back to work. It's only a little tenderness in my side, and I'm sure there's a lot to do to clean up the mess and get things back on track."

Their waitress, Mary, arrived to take their order then. "James!" she said. "Susan! It's wonderful to see you here for lunch. Is everything okay after that terrible explosion? I heard you were caught in it, Susan?" She clutched two menus to her chest like a shield against an unseen attack.

"We're fine, Mary," James said. "Thanks for asking."

"That's good to hear. Do you know what you want today? Do you need menus and a few minutes?" Mary asked her last question with a hint of a smile. James's tendency to always order the same thing was a running joke between the three of them, although James wasn't really amused by it.

"I'll have the usual," James said. "Susan?"

"Oh. Are you in a hurry to get back, James?" Susan asked.

"No, no. I just . . ."

"What are the specials today?" Susan asked, turning to Mary.

"Oh yes, I'm sorry. We have some lobsters from Maine today. So the soup is a bisque, of course. We also have baked lobster with fresh asparagus, and a delicious lobster sandwich with fried potatoes on the side."

"Sounds delicious!" Susan said. "I'll have the soup and the sandwich."

Mary nodded with a wide smile and headed toward the kitchen.

"Lobster?" James said, his lip curling. "Have you had it before?"

"No," Susan said with a grin. "People say it's delicious, though. Even if it's different."

Another couple was sitting a few tables away, closer to the entrance. They were at least a decade older than Susan and James and wearing their Sunday best. The woman wore a burgundy cotton dress, trimmed with lace. The man was in a dark blue suit and a darker navy tie and had a hat perched on one knee. Even though Susan was wearing a skirt and blouse, just as she would for a day at work, she self-consciously straightened her collar.

James peered at Susan through his glasses with a familiar expression on his face.

"What's wrong?" Susan asked.

"Wrong? Nothing. Why?"

"You have the look. Your eyebrows are lopsided. Something is bothering you."

"No. Nothing."

"Fine. Then tell me about the . . . attack." Again, that word. "Do they have any idea who it was?" Susan asked.

"I should think it was obvious," James said with a shrug. "The Black Army probably hates the idea of a national radio network on principle."

"But how would they know to attack us? In Menlo Park?" The question came out automatically before Susan realized she was saying it out loud.

James's eyebrows went out of alignment again. "What do you mean?"

Why had Susan asked that question? Why hadn't she thought about it more before speaking? "How would the Black Army— or anyone else—know that bombing the radio team would stop the project?" she asked.

James sat back in his chair, letting out a long sigh as he held up his arms. "I don't know, Susan. That's not our job, is it? That's up to the SPs and the military."

"Or the press."

"Huh? The press? Did someone talk to you? Let me guess: Carl Urich. Was he in the hospital, planting ideas in your head?"

"Planting ideas in my head? So I can't have my own ideas?"

"That's not what I meant." James put his face in his hands for a moment. "You're right. Whoever planted the bomb must have some knowledge of how the network is being built. But our job is to focus on getting things back on track, not finding the attackers. We need the network for when the Martians finally turn their attention to the Americas."

James was right, of course. They had bigger things to worry about than Carl Urich's paranoid suspicions, but the idea that the reporter had "put ideas in her head" had gotten under Susan's skin.

"The explosion damaged the transmitter unit, but the receivers and power supply are still intact," James continued. "The power supply is the part I was most worried about. We were lucky."

"Lucky?" Susan retorted. "The general's driver wasn't lucky."

"Well, yes. Hopefully, he'll be all right in time. Anyway, we'll be back on track in another day or so. There's no reason for you to rush back to the office. How is your side? You're feeling better?"

"Yes, I am," Susan said, beaming. It had taken James a few minutes, but he had finally asked. He was clearly distracted by the attack at their office. "But I want to go back to work. I can't sit in my room all day. You know me, James."

"Yes, of course. But I want you to be safe."

"Here's your soup, Susan," Mary said, breaking an awkward silence as she skillfully maneuvered a generous portion of bisque onto the table before placing a wooden bowl of salad in front of James. "Enjoy!"

The unnatural silence returned. Susan stirred her bisque, watching the cream swirl without really seeing it. She though to speak a few times, but the words died in her throat. James chewed his salad methodically, his jaw working in a rhythm that seemed almost mechanical. She took a spoonful of soup, and barely tasted it.

Mary returned with Susan's sandwich and James's usual pot roast, with a cheerful "There you are!" that failed to relieve the tension. Susan picked at the sandwich, pulling apart the tender lobster meat with her fork, uncertain how to approach eating it. She was acutely aware of every movement she made—the sound of the bread crust breaking, the scrape of her knife. James cut his food into smaller and smaller pieces, barely eating any of it. The lobster, which had sounded so appealing moments ago, now sat before her like an accusation.

"So," James said after Mary cleared away their lunch dishes in anticipation of coffee, "the attack has made me think, Susan. You're very important to me. The thought of losing you was terrifying, and I think I've taken you for granted."

Susan sat upright in her chair. She and James had been seeing each other for close to five years now, and this kind of talk was distinctly out of character for him.

"Especially after what we went through last year with Colonel Fleming and Sayville," he continued as he reached into the breast pocket of his blazer and produced a small, velvet-covered box, which he opened. "So . . . will you marry me, Susan Wilson?"

The murmur of background conversations dropped away, and time froze. James had proposed. It was the moment Susan had been waiting for, and it had finally arrived.

She opened her mouth to answer but couldn't speak.

James sat across the table, his right hand extended with the open box displaying the ring. It was beautiful, with a stone that glistened in the dim light of the Inn's dining room. Susan worked her mouth to respond and . . .

"Oh my Gawd, Murray, he's proposing!" shouted the woman in the burgundy dress.

James flushed a shade of red that Susan had last seen when he'd forgotten to leave work on time for a play. The woman at the other table leaned in, holding up a hand to hush Murray, who gave no indication that he had anything to say. Mary's face flushed in embarrassment as she walked by with the tray, balancing a bowl of bisque and two sandwiches above her head.

"Yes, James!" Susan said, the words finally coming. "Of course I will marry you!"

"She said yes, Murray!" the woman in burgundy said. "Yes! This is great! See, Murray? Romance ain't dead."

Murray grunted and scooped up some bisque.

James let out a sigh. Had he been worried that Susan might not say yes? She reached out and took his hand across the table.

Mary went back to serving lunches, and the woman in burgundy whispered "Congratulations" to Susan before turning back to Murray.

"I didn't forget my promise," James said. "I was waiting for things to settle down a bit more, but now I know I was waiting for something that wasn't going to happen. There's no time like now."

Susan smiled and squeezed his hand.

"I'm thinking a small ceremony at St. Mark's, and a week down at the shore?" James asked.

"Oh! So you've already thought it all through for us?" It was sweet of him to do that, but Susan had hoped they'd take the time to make plans together. For one thing, she was thinking about Bethlehem Church in Ridgewood, where her parents had married.

"Well," James said, blushing again.

"I'm sorry. Let's enjoy the moment. We'll have plenty of time to plan."

"I was thinking we'd get married right away."

"Right away? You want to be sure you marry me before the Martians kill me?" Where was James's sense of urgency coming from?

His face fell. "This isn't what you want?"

"Of course I want to be married to you. We sat at this very table only a few months ago, and I told you how much I wanted it. But I don't want it to feel like an emergency. We're not getting married because we have to, but because we want to, right?"

"Yes," James said, though he sounded hesitant.

"So let's set a date next week, after I'm back at work. I need to find a dress and talk to my friends." Susan gripped his hand again and added, "I'd like to think about the church a bit, too. Okay?"

"Okay," James said, not looking pleased.

"I'm so happy for you two!" Mary said, walking up with a tray of food. "Here's a special treat to celebrate. It's on the house!"

Susan laughed and smiled as Mary set down the apple pie and coffee for two. She couldn't help but notice that James's smile was forced.

CHAPTER 4

Susan wasn't the kind of worker that watched the clock. Keeping the radio team running, especially after the chaos she'd found when she returned to the office, was satisfying work. But tonight, she would go out for dinner and drinks at Les Halles, her favorite restaurant in nearby Glen Ridge, with Jill and Maggie, two of the other girls who called Mrs. Prendick's boarding house home. Five o'clock couldn't come fast enough.

The week since James had proposed had been a whirlwind. A welcome one, since Susan had had little chance to worry about the office being a target for further attacks, but a whirlwind nonetheless. This Friday night would be her first chance to celebrate a bit, as well as lean on her two best friends to make some plans. For instance, should Susan put her foot down and insist on holding the ceremony in Ridgewood? What kind of dress should she buy? Did she want to go to the shore for a honeymoon? Or somewhere different, like the Adirondacks, or a fancy hotel and a coach ride in the city? She couldn't decide all these issues alone, and the only answer she got from James was, "Whatever's fastest."

He had brought up again the idea of holding a ceremony at

St. Mark's as early as October, but Susan wasn't going to let herself be pressured. You only get married once, after all. Taking a breath and getting it right was the right thing to do.

"Miss Wilson?"

Susan fell out of her reverie and back into the present. The question had come from a second lieutenant who resembled a middle school graduate more than a military academy alum. He had soft blue eyes—the eyes of a boy the army would chew up and spit out—and sandy blond hair that belonged in an elementary school playground.

Susan began, "Yes, that's me, Lieutenant . . .?"

"Boggs, ma'am?" he said, apparently unsure about his own name.

"How can I help you, Lieutenant Boggs?"

"General Ross sent me for the latest report, ma'am? He said you should have it ready?"

"The general is here? So you must be his new driver. Or one of the additional guards the War Department stationed here?"

"His driver, ma'am. And, uh, yes, Miss Wilson—" The lieutenant clenched his fists and sighed. "Sorry. Yes, the general is in the office. And yes, I am his driver, ma'am."

"Relax and take a breath, Lieutenant. And call me Susan." She was a little afraid that he was going to give himself a stroke. "I have the report right here. Is the general feeling okay?"

"Ma'am?"

"Usually, I hear General Ross when he arrives. Is he well? Did he lose his voice?" Susan asked, putting on her best concerned expression.

The lieutenant tilted his head and raised an eyebrow.

"That was a joke, Lieutenant. Do you know how your predecessor is doing? I haven't heard anything about him in a while."

"Uh, he's no longer with us, ma'am," the lieutenant said.

"Oh my God." Tears came to Susan's eyes, and she leaned against her desk, suddenly conscious of the stiffness in her side. She and the driver had been in the room together when the bomb had exploded. She had walked away with some bruised ribs, but he was gone.

"You knew Lieutenant Samuels, ma'am?" Lieutenant Boggs asked.

"Only to say hello. But . . ."

"Oh. That's right. You were here, too. I forgot. You're okay? You weren't hurt?"

"Not that badly. You knew Lieutenant Samuels?"

"Yes. He was two classes ahead of me at VMI." Lieutenant Boggs looked away for a moment. "He helped me a few times."

"I'm sorry. That must be very hard," Susan said, suddenly at a loss for words. She had been feeling sorry for herself, but this man had lost a friend.

"It's a privilege to drive for the general," the lieutenant continued. "But to get the position this way . . ."

"It's not your fault. Maybe you'll bring whoever planted the bomb to justice."

A hint of a smile came to the lieutenant's face. "I didn't think of that. I do get to visit interesting places like the capital, here, and Kearny Point."

"Carny? The general likes carnivals?"

"Oh. I'm not supposed to talk about Kearny." The lieutenant clenched his fists again.

"Talk about what place?" Susan asked with a smile.

The lieutenant's brow crinkled for a moment, then relaxed with understanding. "Thank you," he said as he took the report Susan pulled out of her desk drawer. He gave Susan an awkward half bow and hustled out of her office.

Carny Point? Was it a town? Or a pier? Susan wondered whether she should find a map and familiarize herself with the area. But no time for that. She needed to finish writing up the last inventory before it was time to head out with the girls.

CHAPTER 5

"So tell us everything," Jill said, leaning in as she took a forkful of pasta. Her eyes sparkled mischievously. Jill was a shameless gossip and the closest thing to a best friend Susan had ever had.

Susan laughed. "I already told you everything. James proposed last week. We haven't set a date yet, but he wants it to be soon. I think he would have gone right to the courthouse with me if he'd thought I'd go along with it."

"Why so fast?" Maggie asked. "Weren't you ready to finally dump him a few months ago? You said he wouldn't even talk about setting a date for a wedding. Now he's ready to knock you on the head with a club and drag you before a judge?"

"He said the att—the explosion at Edison made him realize he was taking me for granted," Susan said.

"So he wants to marry you before the Martians get you, huh?" Jill asked with a laugh.

"That's what I said!" Susan exclaimed.

But Maggie wasn't laughing. "I mean it, Susan. Aren't you a little . . ." She trailed off, as if she was afraid to finish her thought. Maggie was always earnest—sometimes a bit too earnest. So, to Susan, her hesitation seemed a bit unlike her.

"Surprised? Shocked? Of course I am." Susan giggled before adding, "If I wasn't, I wouldn't need to lean on my two best friends to help me plan everything right away. James's mother already agreed to go with me to see a dressmaker in Princeton. But I still need a place for the reception."

Maggie's mouth remained in a straight line. "But why this . . . sense of urgency?"

"Can't you be happy for her, Maggie?" Jill asked with another laugh. "She's getting married! To someone she likes and who actually has a future. Before you know it, she'll be inviting us over to a little house down the lane to watch her three kids!"

"Three kids!" Susan said, her eyes wide with shock. "I'm still looking for a wedding dress, and you have me barefoot and pregnant in the kitchen!"

Maggie smiled, but it didn't reach her eyes.

Susan extended her hand and took Maggie's. "You really are worried, aren't you? Look, James and I have been through a lot the past eight months, and he realized he doesn't want to wait any longer. Understand? It's as simple as that."

Maggie sighed. "You're right. I have no right to question his motives." She lowered her gaze for a moment before continuing. "So, have they learned anything about the bombing? Was it the Germans? The same people who tried to kill James in that explosion in Coney Island?"

Susan wanted to tell her friends what had actually happened in Coney Island. She wanted to explain how close James had come to being killed there by Martian sympathizers, not German agents. How she and James had nearly walked into a firefight between those sympathizers and the Black Army in Manhattan. How the explosion at Edison was a strike against the nascent National Radio Network. But only a handful of people knew about the Martian conspiracy, and the Security Police had made what would happen to Susan—and her friends—abundantly clear if she told them.

"James has been great for you," Maggie continued before

Susan could answer, "and you deserve the wedding you want. Let's take a train to Ridgewood this weekend and find the perfect spot for your reception. I'm friends with a few members of the Woman's Club. They have a beautiful spot a few blocks from the church."

"Wonderful!" Susan said, clapping her hands.

"I think going along with his mother on your dress would go a long way toward making people happy," Jill said. "But that doesn't mean you can't pick out his tuxedo."

"I like the way you think, Jill," Susan said. "Devious and—"

"That's it, everyone!" said a deep voice from behind Susan. "Time to go home!"

Susan spun around and saw three men, all dressed in the black leather of the Security Police and brandishing pistols.

"What's going on?" asked a man from somewhere behind the SPs.

"What's 'going on' is orders from President Bryan," one of the SPs answered sternly. "There will be a local curfew of eight p.m. until the terrorists who have been violating the peace are captured. Go home. Now."

"A curfew?" someone else shouted from the far end of the room. "At eight p.m.? Why do we have to suffer because you can't find the bombers? Do your job, and leave us alone!"

One of the SPs muttered obscenities as he and a comrade charged toward the heckler.

Maggie shivered. "I hope they catch whoever attacked your office soon."

Attacked.

"Sending us home at 8:00 p.m. won't catch anyone," Jill said, rolling her eyes.

"Ssshhhh! They might hear you!" Maggie whispered. "We'd better go before they get upset with us, too." She nodded at the heckler, who was being restrained by two of the officers.

Susan knew that Jill was right. Nearly all the bombings that were a fact of life since the beginning of the year had been during the day and in public areas. Carl Urich had pointed this out when Susan had met him in town last week. This curfew was about control, not about making people safer. But it was easy to see why Maggie was intimidated by the SPs: They wanted her to be afraid, and she didn't know how corrupt and inept they were, and Susan couldn't tell her without revealing too much.

"Let's settle the bill at the door and go home," Susan said.

CHAPTER 6

"It looks like the guys at GE will come through with those voltage regulators," Noah Abrams said with a broad smile as he hung up his desk phone. "Heaven knows how they've been producing components so quickly, but that'll shut the general up. At least for a few minutes."

"I'm sure I can think of something to say, Abrams," General Ross said as he stepped into the room.

Noah's face turned ashen. He stood up and stuttered a weak apology.

"Sit down, Abrams. Oh, and *you* can shut up," the general said before he turned to Susan. Where's your other half?" he asked.

Susan blinked in confusion.

"Brogan. Where's Brogan? The man you're going to marry. Remember him?"

Heat rose in Susan's face. Her other half? She and James hadn't set a date yet, but the general was already reducing her to half a person. It wasn't a surprise, of course. In fact, it was typical. Susan was the only woman at Edison who didn't carry a mop or work on a factory floor, and comments about where she should be instead of behind a desk were not unusual. But listening to the general shove her into James's shadow rankled her.

"I don't know, sir," Susan said as she checked her watch. It read 9:15 a.m. James was late again. Would she end up late all the time when they moved in together? Or would she have to drag him to the office by nine?

"Well, maybe having you at home will straighten him out," the general said with a chuckle.

What was that supposed to mean? Did General Ross think she was going to stay home and manage James's schedule for him? Susan considered asking, but she elected to take a different tack, since the general seemed chatty.

"So we have a new curfew, General," she said. "Does that mean there're no leads on the bombing? Do they still think it's the Black Army?"

"No leads, according to what I've heard," General Ross said with a grunt. Did he remember that someone had nearly killed him last week?

"The Security Police chased me and my friends home at eight o'clock last night. We barely had time to finish our dinner, let alone have a drink."

The general shrugged. "They're only trying to make sure everyone's safe."

Everyone except the man they beat and dragged out in handcuffs, in other words. Susan didn't say that, but she wasn't ready to accept the general's platitudes. He had connections in the SPs and the Bryan administration. He had to know more.

"But a curfew feels more like theater than a solution, doesn't it?" Susan asked. "This office might be a target for someone who's not happy with the radio network. Shouldn't we do more than post a few guards outside?" She looked to Noah for support, but he stared back like she was juggling hand grenades while singing the German national anthem.

"How did the attackers know to plant a bomb here?" she

added. "What was their goal? Either there's something the SPs aren't telling us, or—"

"Something they're not telling us?" the general growled. "Like what? Where is this coming from? Has Brogan been having doubts? Have you been talking to the press? And what do a bunch of girls need to be doing out alone after eight at night, anyway? We'll have a curfew until we find out what the hell's going on."

"And that's a good thing," said James as he entered the office bearing a white wax paper bakery bag. "You've already had enough close calls, honey. It's not safe out there."

Susan reeled back in her chair. James was siding with the general? After he had implied that she couldn't possibly have come up with these questions herself? How could he?

"Not safe out *there*?" she said, fighting to keep her voice level. "The bomb was *here*, James. Not in a restaurant or a department store. Here. In a building that was already supposed to be secure."

"Now see here, young lady," the general said, pointing at Susan.

Had General Ross really just "young ladied" her? Susan spun around to face him, but James cut her off with a proffered cup of coffee.

"Here," James said, smiling nervously. "I brought you this from the bakery." He produced an apple fritter from the bag.

"You have time for shopping on your way to work, Brogan?" the general growled. Susan knew she hadn't done James any favors by setting General Ross off, but he deserved it after showing up late and kissing up to the ogre.

"Actually, Seward and I were here past midnight last night, sir," James said. "But we finished, General. We're ready to test the network."

The general almost smiled. "Well, it's about time."

"We were testing with the receivers Noah got in from GE last week, and part of the problem was with them. They're not reliable, sir. They need to improve their build standards. Maybe we should go speak to GE?"

"Well, uh, we don't have time for that right now, Brogan. What's next?"

"We can ship the transmitters to the broadcast station in Manhattan this afternoon."

"Ship? No." General Ross pulled a cigar out from his jacket pocket as he added, "You and Seward get them loaded onto a truck here and drive them out there yourselves. Now."

"It would be better if you smoked outside or in one of the labs, General," Susan said. "Mr. Abrams is allergic to the smoke."

"Oh, that's okay," Noah said. "I can handle it."

Of course he'd say that. Susan didn't handle the smoke well herself. But any complaint from her would fall on deaf ears.

"Hmmmph." The general flashed an icy look toward Susan as he followed James out of the office. "Show me your handiwork, Brogan, and we can finish our plans in the lab."

"We're ready to go," James said when he returned to Susan's office around noon. "Seward was able to pick up a signal over in West Orange, with the transmitter just using a six-foot aerial!"

"That's great," Susan said without looking up from her typewriter.

James offered a hopeful grin. "Time for lunch, then?"

"I guess."

"What's wrong?" James asked. The man had the memory of a goldfish.

"What's wrong?" Susan answered. "You weren't even here for two minutes this morning before you were backing the general and patronizing me about the curfew."

James was silent for a minute. "I'm sorry."

"Are you?"

"I just said—"

"I heard what you said, James. But are you?" Susan stood as she asked the last question. Her heart was beating faster, and a single bead of sweat ran down her forehead. When James had arrived earlier, she had only wanted to make sure he was aware he'd hurt her feelings, but this was about more than that. "You walked in here, dismissed what I said before you even greeted me and then promptly forgot it happened," she added.

"I was distracted by the general and the transmitters—"

"The general and his transmitters. Like nothing is more important than that." Susan held up a hand as she struggled for words. She was so tired of hearing about those transmitters, and now James was using them as an excuse? "Propaganda delivery system."

James raised an eyebrow. "Propaganda delivery system? Was the general right? Have you been talking to Urich?" A half smile crept onto his face as he spoke.

"You too? Is it so hard to believe that I can have ideas of my own?" Susan asked, struggling yet again to keep her voice level. She didn't need to be labeled as "hysterical," on top of being a parrot.

"It does sound like him."

"So it can't possibly be an original thought. At least not from a woman, right?"

"I didn't say that."

"What do you think these radios are for? Don't you wonder why they pulled you off reproducing the weapons those German soldiers created to fight the Martians?"

"You mean the radioflash? We didn't need that."

"Because the Martians aren't here yet? So what will happen when they show up? Will President Bryan lull them to sleep with one of his speeches about the Bible?"

James worked his mouth, then shrugged.

Was Susan being unreasonable? Or was James really so thoughtless? Either way, she needed some distance from him before she said something she couldn't take back.

"Go," she said, pointing to the door.

James opened his mouth to say something, but Susan shook her head and kept her finger pointed at the door. Eventually, James left.

Susan waited a full fifteen minutes before heading to the lunchroom, just to be sure she didn't run into him.

CHAPTER 7

Susan scanned the newspaper as she sat behind her desk. The headlines had caught her eye when she had picked the paper up at the Edison office's front door, so she had held onto it to take a look before putting it back in the break room.

CHAOS IN EUROPE

While the governments in Belgium, France, and Germany seem to be all but lost, pockets of fighting between man and Martian are reported in Prussia, Saxony, and the Alsace. At the same time, in northern France and Belgium . . .

Would the network do anything to protect the United States from the inevitable Martian attack? Carl's words about "falling back on a comfortable lie" haunted Susan. It might be time to learn whether Captain Reynolds in Sayville knew something.

General Ross and James had spent most of the past couple of weeks in New York City, setting up the broadcast center for the radios. Of course, James didn't know what the SPs and the Bryan administration planned for the network, and the general might not know, either. That wasn't his purview. But James had been too infatuated with the idea of "his" radios broadcasting across the nation to discuss what the programming itself might contain.

Another headline caught Susan's eye as she put the newspaper down: "MORE MYSTERIOUS DISAPPEARANCES. POLICE SILENT."

Carl Urich had mentioned something about disappearances when Susan had run into him by 'Wicks. Was this what he had meant? He'd implied that he'd given up on the story to follow the bombing here. But why? The story reported that hundreds of people had disappeared from the slums surrounding the site of the Tesla fire. That sounded ominous. And, of course, the New York City Police had nothing to say about it. Were they covering something up? Or did they not care about the slums?

"Good morning!" Noah Abrams said as he walked into the office.

"Good morning, Noah," Susan said. "You're a little early today."

"Well, the general will be in today, so . . ." Noah let his voice trail off for dramatic effect.

Susan laughed.

"So what did you learn yesterday?" Noah asked.

"April is our best bet," Susan said.

With James and the general away, she had taken the day off and traveled to Ridgewood to talk to the church and the reception hall. She'd found a couple of weekends in April where both venues would be free. Now it was time for her to convince James to set a realistic date, rather than him pressuring her to run off to the courthouse like a pair of teenagers in trouble.

"Sounds good. Plenty of time for you to prepare. How's the place your friend Maggie mentioned? The Ladies' Club?"

"Woman's Club, you mean. It's perfect. It's walking distance from the church, like Maggie said. It's a lovely old place. Very traditional, just like my mom would have liked. It won't be too expensive, either."

"That's great!"

"Yes. Now if I can convince James to slow down and settle on a reasonable date, it'll all work out," Susan said. "We're going to dinner tonight to discuss it."

"I'm sure he's in a rush because he's worried you'll change your mind," Noah said with a chuckle.

But was that it? Was James really that insecure? Or was something else going on? Getting married was supposed to be a happy occasion, not one filled with mystery and anxiety.

Just seconds before nine o'clock that morning, James strode into Susan's office sporting a three-day-old beard and a wrinkled shirt.

"Whoa! Did you get any sleep at all last night?" Susan asked.

"A few hours," James answered. "The president wants the entire network up before the end of October. We have the transmitters for New York up and running, but the relays out west are giving us trouble. I need to take the train out to Philadelphia with a power supply and a tuner. If that works, I might not have to go to Chicago. I can send instructions to the GE engineers over there."

Susan's heart sank. Not only was their dinner—and her plans—now in jeopardy, but also the general was working James nearly to death. "This is ridiculous," she said. "You might not make it to Pennsylvania, let alone Illinois, if you don't let yourself rest."

"I can sleep on the train."

"James, we're supposed to have dinner tonight. I want to talk about the wedding. I have some dates for the church and the reception."

James sighed and stared at his feet. "I don't know why it has to be so complicated. We can get married after I'm finished with the network. We can have your friends, my mother, and—"

Susan's chest tightened. Once she caught her breath, it was her turn to sigh, but with enough feeling that she noticed Noah getting up from his desk and discreetly leaving the office.

"James, we're not going to run to the county clerk like a couple of kids," Susan said. "I want to be married in the same church as my parents. Why is that too much to ask? It's available in April, and so is the perfect place for the reception. That's only a few months off."

James lifted his gaze to Susan, his eyes wide with shock. "April? But I already found a house for us. It's right off Pleasant Valley Way—"

Susan's mouth dropped open in astonishment. "You've been looking at houses? Without me? Before we've set a date?" She backed up and sat down before she fell over from shock. "What . . . what is going on with you, James? You don't have time for dinner with me, but you've had time to find us a house?" Her voice rose with each sentence, but she didn't care if she made a scene.

"Calm down," James said as he closed the office door. "We should talk about this later."

"Calm down? I'm upset because we *can't* talk about it later, like we planned. Because you're too busy building President Bryan's network and deciding where I'm going to live."

"That's not what I'm doing."

"Then what are you doing? Why would you go house hunting without talking to me? Why are you burning the candle at both ends for a propaganda network? And how are you in a hurry to get married when you don't even have time for dinner?"

James was silent. Clamming up under pressure was his specialty, and Susan knew it would take some pushing to get a reaction out of him.

"I don't have any choice about the radios," James said. "If we don't finish on time, we could lose our position with the government. We could be accused of trying to sabotage the project."

"But earlier this year, we uncovered a major conspiracy in the SPs and saved countless lives. You think they're going to throw you in jail for getting some sleep? Do you think you're helping the project if you're too exhausted to think straight?"

"What we did a few months ago doesn't matter, Susan. You know that. You're aware of how quickly they turned on Mr. Johnson."

Susan winced at the mention of Ben's name. "Don't bring him into this! What do you think he'd say about this radio network?"

James paused before answering. "Maybe the fact that he'd resist it is why he's gone."

Shock ran through Susan's body. She'd assumed that whoever was behind the conspiracy to make the United States an easier target for the Martians had kidnapped and killed him, too. "So he deserved what he got?" she growled.

"No! Of course not. But he stuck out. He attracted attention to himself."

"Oh, I see. He didn't deserve it, but he asked for it."

James sighed again. He was clearly exhausted, and Susan wondered whether that might have been why he'd come close to blaming Ben Johnson for his own murder. But it didn't excuse his going out and picking out a home for her. It was 1915, not 1815!

Susan crossed her arms before speaking again. "This is pointless. If you don't want to have dinner tonight, that's up to you. But understand this: I'm not getting married this month, or next month. I'm never getting married in a courthouse. I'm also not going to move into a house that someone else picked for me. I'm already a guest in a rooming house. I don't plan on moving from one to another."

James's brow furrowed. Before he could reply, the general yelled from down the hall. "Brogan! Where the hell are you?"

Susan opened her office door to let James out before she said something she would regret.

The rest of the day crawled to the five o'clock finish line. Noah, picking up on Susan's mood, had said nothing after returning to the office. James never came back, so Susan felt it was safe to assume he'd left for Philadelphia without saying goodbye. Typical. He was skilled at avoiding difficult conversations.

Susan took her purse and hat with her to the break room so that she could leave from there after cleaning up whatever mess the engineers had left. Workers had just replaced the wall between the break room and the lab, but the Buildings Department had taken advantage of the situation and added a door between the two rooms. James and the other engineers didn't like the idea, because it meant losing wall space in the lab, but Edison's corporate offices had gone ahead with the project.

And it *was* a project. While Susan had been recuperating, the carpenters had left a door-sized hole when they'd rebuilt the wall. They'd added a frame a few days later, then mumbled something about not having any doors to install and left. Susan had picked up the baton when she'd returned; after a week, the carpenters had come back and hung a canvas tarp between the two rooms.

Susan was thinking about this when she heard General Ross speak from the other side of the doorway, inside the lab. "I thought you were already gone!" he said.

"I was," Susan heard James reply, "but I forgot the oscillograph."

Susan dropped the rag she'd been using to wipe down the counter when he heard James speak. He wasn't gone yet? He was going to end up on a late train if he wasn't careful. But at least he might get some sleep during the trip to Philadelphia.

"I swear to God, boy," the general said. "You'd forget your head if it wasn't sewn on."

"I'm sorry, sir. I'm just a little tired."

"And distracted. I don't know why you don't lay down the law with that girl."

"I know, sir, but—"

"No buts. I told you to get her out of the office. She's not safe, and I can't have you worrying about her if we go to war with the Martians."

"I'm working on it. It's just that . . ."

The world seemed to go white around Susan as the words fell into place. *Get her out of the office. She's not safe. I'm working on it.* This was where James's sense of urgency was coming from. He was following orders. General Ross must have told James to get rid of her, and James's solution was to marry her and leave her at home.

Susan stormed into the lab before she realized she'd moved at all. General Ross and James were standing on either side of a workbench, both struck dumb by her appearance.

"Susan, I . . ." James sputtered.

"Shut up," she said. "You proposed to me because you were following orders? To get me out of the office?"

"No, I—"

"I said shut up," Susan repeated. "Well, I have excellent news for you and the general. I'm out of the office, and you don't have to marry me. As a matter of fact, you're *not* marrying me."

She pulled the ring off her finger and threw it at James. Then she reached into her purse, pulled out her keys, slipped off the key to the Edison office's front door, and threw it after her ring.

As Susan headed out the door of Edison for the last time, she realized James—either because he was too dumbstruck, tired, or afraid—hadn't followed her.

CHAPTER 8

lock-watching was becoming a habit for Susan. Of course, just a day ago, she'd been watching the clock because she couldn't wait to leave the office. This time, her eyes were fixed on her watch because she wasn't at work. She was out of work—literally and figuratively—and sitting at 'Wicks, waiting for Jill to show up for lunch.

Had anyone seen the crazy-looking lady crying as she had lurched from Edison's Menlo Park office to Mrs. Prendick's boarding house yesterday? Susan hoped not. But as terrible as that possibility was, she had bigger problems. What was she going to do now? She'd spent most of the night lying in bed, repeating the question. But neither she nor the thirty-five tiny plaster cracks in her ceiling had answers.

"More coffee, Susan?" Penny asked, stirring Susan out of her woolgathering.

"Oh! No thanks, Penny, I'm ready to float home as it is. My friend will be here soon."

Penny smiled, nodded, and went back to waiting tables.

Susan turned back toward the door, willing Jill to finally arrive. She had enough savings that she didn't need to worry about finding work right away. After the Martians had killed her parents in the first attack, her Aunt Margaret had sold their house and banked the proceeds for when Susan turned eighteen. By then, Susan was already working in an office, and she hadn't needed to touch any of that money yet.

While losing her parents at age six had been traumatic, Susan knew she had been lucky. Her aunt had provided a loving home for her, made it possible for her to stay in her hometown, and set money aside for her future. Initially, Susan had been sad that her mother's older sister wasn't still alive to see her wedding. But now, with the wedding off and her life in tatters, Susan missed Aunt Margaret more than ever.

She wiped away a tear and scanned the diner. A kindly-looking older man in a mail carrier's uniform. An unfriendly woman wearing a ridiculous hat. A teenage boy who checked the door even more frequently than Susan.

Susan yawned. Maybe she did need more coffee. She raised a hand for Penny's attention, then mimed drinking from her mug. Penny grinned and indicated she'd be right there.

The mail carrier rose, waved to Penny, and exited 'Wicks, leaving a five-cent tip and a newspaper behind. Susan stood as Penny arrived with the coffeepot.

"Do you still want more coffee?" Penny asked.

"Yes, please," Susan replied. "I was going to grab that newspaper, if that's all right."

"Of course. Mr. Newell leaves one behind every day, and I let it stay out for whoever wants to read it, although I tease Mr. Urich that no one does."

"Oh. Is it *The Spectator*?"

"The only paper Mr. Newell will read," Penny said as she filled Susan's mug.

Susan returned to her seat with the paper and spread it out on the table before adding milk and sugar to her coffee. The lead story was about the *Mauretania*, a British ocean liner that had disappeared somewhere in the northern Atlantic on its way to Nova Scotia. The United States and British governments claimed to be investigating the possibility of an iceberg being responsible, similar to the *Titanic* disaster, but the article hinted at Martian involvement. Susan checked the article's byline. Carl Urich.

The story below the fold was about the continuing disappearances in New York City. While most of the missing were factory workers, immigrants, and other folk who lived south of the site of the Tesla fire, the daughter of a prominent lawyer was missing now, and people were asking questions. But wasn't that always the case? A bunch of poor people would go missing, and no one would care. Then one young lady from a respectable family would disappear, and it would become one of the biggest stories of the day.

Of course, Ben Johnson's disappearance hadn't earned any attention either, Susan noted. It was a national security matter, according to the Security Police. Ben had access to information about government projects and, of course, the Long Island radio towers that had been the target of the conspiracy Susan and James had uncovered. But it didn't explain why his disappearance had to be kept secret. General Ross had brushed Susan off every time she'd asked him about Ben. He was too busy conspiring with James to get her barefoot and pregnant in the kitchen to spend any time or effort on that mystery.

Heat rose in Susan's face. She fought back a sob as she folded the paper and put it aside. Enough with the news for now.

"Are you okay?" Jill asked as she approached the table. "You look awful."

"Thanks," Susan said.

"Anything for you, my love," Jill quipped, never missing a beat. "Seriously, though. How are you doing?"

Jill had been home from her job at the hair salon yesterday when Susan had stumbled into the boarding house, blubbering like a schoolgirl who had just found out her crush was dating the head cheerleader. She'd shepherded Susan upstairs, brewed chamomile tea, and fended off Maggie so that Susan wouldn't have to hear "I told you so." At least not yet.

"Surprisingly well," Susan said with a wan smile. "I have no idea what I'm going to do next. But at the same time, I am appreciating the things I won't be doing."

Jill raised an eyebrow. "You've been through a lot."

"I know . . . and I didn't say I was okay. I said I am doing surprisingly well."

"Well, if you need anything while you figure out what is next, I'm here. I've saved up plenty of tips."

"I can support myself for the foreseeable future, but thank you."

"And you've heard nothing yet from James?"

Susan scoffed. "He's working. He made it clear where his priorities lie. I imagine he'll show up tomorrow or the day after."

"And you'll . . ." Jill let her voice trail off, extending a hand to indicate that Susan should complete her sentence.

"Tell him to go away," Susan said with a shrug.

Jill smiled.

"I know what to stay away from. It's where I want to go that's the issue." Susan absentmindedly picked up the newspaper before adding, "Things were so much easier last year, when Ben Johnson was still around."

"Your old boss?" Jill asked. "You never told me what happened to him. Why would you be thinking about him now? Was something going on? Did you not tell me?"

Susan's eyes opened wide as she stared back at Jill. "Something going on? My God, Jill. He was nearly old enough to be my father!"

"Here you go, ladies," said Penny as she placed menus in front of Jill and Susan. "Do you need a moment to think about what you want?"

"Pancakes, two eggs over easy, bacon, and toast," Jill said. "And give me a cup of coffee, and make sure it never gets empty.

I've got half the Ladies Auxiliary coming to my chair at the salon today."

"I'll have two eggs, bacon, and rye toast," said Susan.

Penny left before Jill said, "So he was a bit older. That can be fun."

"That's not how it was," Susan said. Could she risk cluing Jill in? Would it endanger her? If there was one person she could trust with a secret, it was Jill.

Susan glanced right and left, like a spy preparing to divulge their secrets in a dark bar, then told her story. She started with James's fateful trip to the radio towers in Sayville and how it nearly got him killed in Coney Island.

"He was at Dreamland when that bomb killed those marines?" Jill whispered in shock.

Penny interrupted with their food, then Susan continued all the way through to the search for a rogue transmitter in Manhattan that triggered a shoot-out at the Metropolitan Life Building.

"There weren't any newspaper stories about that," Jill hissed, struggling to keep her voice down.

"It was easy to cover up, since there were almost no witnesses," Susan said. "The SPs certainly wanted to, since some of their men were involved on the wrong side. They even still have access to the site where the transmitter was running."

Jill's mouth gaped open.

"Your eggs are getting cold," Susan said.

"You went through all that and never told me?"

"I was sworn to secrecy. If the wrong people find out I told you, our best outcome would be to share a cell."

"I get the cute prison guard."

"We'd have female guards."

Jill shrugged. "I hear prison does get pretty lonely."

Susan giggled.

"So what about this Captain Reynolds who helped you and James?" Jill asked after finishing a bite of pancake.

"What about him?" Susan asked.

"He sounds like a reliable guy," Jill said as she sliced her pancakes. "He might know something about what happened to your old boss."

Susan took a bite of toast. The odds that Reynolds knew much were low, but he might have an idea of who to ask, if nothing else. But then what? "He might, but so what?" she asked.

"Well, then you'd find out. You might get some peace, at least with respect to what happened to him. You can't just put on your Sunday best and start interviewing for a new job, Susan. You need some time to recover. But you're not going to sit here and read the paper for the rest of 1915. I know you. You need something to do."

Jill was right. Susan had been through a lot over the past few months, and taking some time before she jumped into whatever the next phase of her life was going to look like was what she needed. But trying to uncover something the government didn't want revealed wasn't exactly healing, was it?

Then again, could Susan recover if she didn't learn what had happened to Ben?

"I think you're right," Susan said.

CHAPTER 9

The trip from West Orange to Sayville took longer than Susan expected. She had to catch a train near home and take it to Hoboken. From there, she switched to a subway under the Hudson into New York City. She was familiar with that part of the journey. She'd traveled to New York many times for theater, parties, and shopping. The city was one of her favorite places, and she'd seriously considered relocating there a few times—even as recently as January, when she'd initially quit Edison because Sean Fleming had replaced Ben Johnson as head of Edison's radio team.

The tricky part of the trip was the hop from New York City to Long Island. Subways didn't go all the way to Sayville, so Susan needed to catch a train from Pennsylvania Station. These trains, which ran through a new tunnel under the East River, were for workers who lived on Long Island, so trips back to the island during the day were sporadic at best.

But Susan wasn't in a hurry. There was no way she'd arrive early enough to invite Reynolds to lunch, so either she was going to have to talk to him at the radio towers or she would get there late enough for dinner or a drink. So she got off the train from New Jersey at Christopher Street and climbed to the street where, hanging on the wall leading out of the stairwell, was a familiar sight:

**CURFEW: 22:00 HOURS
PUNISHABLE BY $15 FINE AND JAIL
BY ORDER OF THE SECURITY POLICE**

A similar warning had been hanging in Midtown when Susan had last visited New York City with James. That had been the night they'd found a rogue transmitter interfering with the Planetary Warning System. It had also been the last time she'd spoken to Reynolds in person.

The station on Christopher Street was close enough to the river for auras of salt water, fresh fish, and coal smoke, to fill the air. But those fragrances faded into the smells of baked bread, horse, and—of course—trash as Susan headed north on Hudson Street and Manhattan's shoreline angled away from her. One of the reasons she decided to walk was the bohemian hustle and bustle of Greenwich Village. It was, in many ways, the polar opposite of West Orange. She loved relaxed lunches at Renwick's and would miss her dinners with James at the Inn, but that was all her adopted hometown had to offer. But one would be hard-pressed to sample all the different restaurants, bars, cafés, and bakeries packed into the four blocks of the Village.

Susan had just crossed Jane Street when a dark-skinned man handed her a colorful flyer. "Where are they?" the young man said. "Where are the missing? Why doesn't Mayor Gettys care?" He was wearing a threadbare suit and jacket despite the summer heat, and he clutched a sheaf of flyers under his left arm like he was afraid someone would try to take them away.

"The missing?" Susan asked.

Her query stunned the young man, probably because he was

used to people refusing the papers or scurrying away from him as fast as their feet would go. "Yes, the missing. Have you heard about them?"

"If you mean the people missing from downtown, yes. I'm actually—I read about it in *The Spectator*."

"Yes, them," the young man said. "They might be the only paper that's been covering the story. My cousin disappeared a few days ago. The police wouldn't even talk to my uncle!"

"Oh, that's terrible," Susan said.

"Is this man bothering you, miss?" asked a deep voice from behind Susan. She turned to face a tall man dressed like he had just come off the docks. "Shove off, boy," he said to the man with the flyers. "She doesn't want whatever you're selling."

"We're friends, thank you," Susan said as evenly as she could.

"Oh, one of those," the deep-voiced man growled, then stomped off.

Susan turned back to face the young man. "I'm sorry," she said, feeling obligated to apologize for him.

"Not your fault, ma'am," he said with an expression that told Susan this hadn't been his first time.

Susan read the flyer, smoothing out creases she must have made when the deep-voiced man had become upset and she'd clenched her hands. "You have regular meetings? At Redeemer Baptist Church?"

"Yes, ma'am. Every Thursday. Down on Jackson Street, near the water."

"I really hope you find your cousin," Susan said, not knowing what else to say.

"Thanks again, ma'am," the young man said with a sad smile.

At the train station in Sayville, Susan smiled when she saw three hansom cabs waiting for passengers. Sayville was predominantly a fishing town, but she had hoped it saw enough traffic, especially with the nearby ferry service to Fire Island, that she would find a ride to her destination. "Radio towers, please," she said to one of the drivers.

"Fifty cents," he said.

Susan froze in surprise before reaching into her purse for change. Fifty cents! That was a New York City rate. Well, it was already four o'clock, and the towers were a mile away. She nodded and climbed into the cab. The driver climbed up to his seat and started the ride.

Susan had found a beautiful copy of *The Turn of the Screw* in a used bookstore in Chelsea and read a few chapters on the train. But based on the rough ride as she left the train station, trying to read in the cab would be futile and frustrating. She opened her purse to put the book away, and the flyer from the young man in Greenwich Village caught her eye. How could hundreds of people simply disappear? Why wouldn't the police help? How was this story not important enough for the *Times* or the *Post*?

The twin masts of the radio station had already been visible from the train, but they dominated the view as the cab approached the station. Susan had never been to Sayville before, but she'd seen photos of the antennas and James had described the station so many times that she felt as if she had visited it before. Soon, a steel fence topped with menacing barbed wire came into view. The marines had taken over the station the previous year and turned it into a military installation. James had complained bitterly about the takeover a few times, even after he'd worked with the marines to bring the systems back online.

Susan's heart climbed into her throat. The marines! This wasn't an Edison installation now; it was a military camp. Would they let her in?

The cab pulled up in front of a gate and guardhouse. Susan climbed out and paid the driver. She turned to approach the guardhouse and found herself facing a pair of uniformed guards.

One held a clipboard; the other, a rifle. Susan clenched her hands to conceal their shaking.

"Can I help you, ma'am?" the clipboard-wielding marine asked.

"Yes, I'm here to see Captain Reynolds," Susan said, hoping the waver in her voice wasn't too obvious.

"Who are you?" the marine asked.

"Susan Wilson. The captain knows me from Edison." Susan saw no reason to mention that she didn't work there anymore.

"Do you have an appointment?"

"Uh." Dammit. "No, I don't."

Clipboard Marine looked at Rifle Marine, who shrugged and checked his watch.

"You said Edison?" Clipboard Marine asked. "Can I see your identification?"

Susan started to say no, then realized she had identification. She'd thrown the keys to the office at James, but she had forgotten to surrender her employee card. The marines wouldn't know it was invalid. Would they?

She reached into her purse, pulled out her wallet, and opened it to show Clipboard Marine the card. He examined it and raised his eyes to meet Susan's. "I need you to take it out and hand it to me, ma'am."

Susan remembered a story she'd read about Black Army soldiers getting into an actual army camp with forged paperwork. Was Clipboard Marine going to verify her employment? Was she lying her way into a prison cell? It wasn't too late to excuse herself, but she needed to find out what happened to Ben Johnson. Maybe she would find out firsthand what they'd done to him.

Susan pulled the card out of the wallet and dropped it because of her sweaty, shaking hands. She froze, staring at the card lying in the gravel driveway. Clipboard Marine bent down, picked the card up, and examined it for seconds that passed like hours.

"Looks fine," he finally said, and Susan exhaled loudly enough that she thought she had given herself away. Nevertheless, Clipboard Marine nodded to Rifle Marine and gestured to Susan. "I'll take you to the office, ma'am."

The door to the station opened into an office, where operators hunched over telegraph controls and microphones. Clipboards hung in a row across the far wall, bearing unintelligible notation that had more in common with the shorthand Susan was relieved she'd never had to use at Edison than any human language. The air was thick with smoke from cheap cigars and stale cigarettes. How did James, with his intense dislike of smoke, stand it?

"Susan Wilson!" Reynolds said, craning his neck to see around Susan as she entered the main room in the radio tower office. "You're up and about after that explosion? What brings you all the way out here? Is Brogan with you?"

"Uh, no," Susan said. "I'm alone. I was wondering if we could talk?"

The captain raised his eyebrows, then nodded in understanding. "Sure. Let's step outside."

He led Susan outside and headed away from the building and the guardhouse. "Are you okay?" he asked when they were out of earshot from the guards. "What brings you all the way out here for a private conversation? Did something happen to Brogan?"

"James is fine," Susan said. "Well, as far as I know, he is."

Reynolds tilted his head but said nothing.

"I'm actually here to see if you know anything about Ben Johnson," Susan continued. "About what happened to him."

The captain's forehead wrinkled. "What happened . . . ?" he asked.

"All I've heard is that he disappeared. Is that really all the government knows? Have you heard anything else? I hoped you might know more, or whether there's someone you can ask."

"You're asking me for information the SPs don't want you to have?"

Susan frowned as she and Reynolds stopped near the corner of the compound furthest from the entrance gate. This wasn't working. She had wasted her time traveling all the way to Long Island—and on top of that, she was risking getting herself, the captain, and even his men in trouble.

Reynolds crossed his arms, but he still had a concerned expression on his face. "I don't know you very well, Miss Wilson, but I can tell something is troubling you. Have you heard something new about Johnson? He disappeared a few days after the explosion on Coney Island, but that's all I know. What's going on?"

"I-I can't believe that he just disappeared without a trace. No body? No one saw him on the train? No last known location? Sean Fleming played a big part in the conspiracy while he was part of the SPs. How do we know that some of the people working with him aren't still around?"

"Have you discussed this with Brogan? Or General Ross? Ross has friends in the SPs."

An unexpected wave of anger came over Susan at the sound of the general's name. She'd worked hard to avoid thinking about him or James. "Yes, he has friends in the SPs. That's why I wouldn't believe a word he said—if he was willing to talk about Ben Johnson. He's why I left Edison!" She let that last statement slip out before she could help herself.

"Left Edison? You're not working for them "?" Reynolds said, his voice rising with each word. He paused, then took a deep breath. "What are you doing here? How did you get past my guards?"

"Please don't blame them. I forgot to turn in my identification when I walked out. It's my fault."

"Are you insane?" Reynolds hissed. "Walking into a secure

compound with invalid identification? They've locked people up and thrown away the key for less. And what about my men? Do you think they'd get by with anything less than a court-martial?"

Susan gazed at her shoes, not sure what to say.

"And Ross," Reynolds continued. "I expected better from him. Although the scuttlebutt is that he's under a lot of pressure with the public network." He crossed his arms again and held Susan's gaze for a moment.

"But I need to get you out of here before we both end up in front of an SP magistrate," he said as he checked his watch. "I'd better escort you out of here and all the way to Sayville, just to be sure you don't come back."

CHAPTER 10

want to be clear, Miss Wilson," Reynolds said as he and Susan sat down at a pub in downtown Sayville. "I brought you here because I want to help you, not as a reward for entering my station under false pretenses."

Susan surveyed the pub the captain had led her to. It had a rustic charm but was indeed no reward. The walls were white-washed—or, rather, graywashed—and trimmed with aged timbers from at least a hundred years earlier. The floor bore a sticky sheen from years of wet boots, spilled beer, and assorted bodily fluids. The sparse clientele, who were all men, sported tattoos, scars, and the practical garments of fishers, farmers, and tradespeople. It reminded Susan of the bar in Midtown, where she'd met Reynolds. "I understand," she said, "and I'm grateful, Captain. Please, call me Susan."

A waitress arrived and took their orders. Susan opted for the same beer and shepherd's pie the captain ordered.

"So, tell me what's been going on," he said once the waitress left.

Susan told her story, starting with the explosion. She took an extra moment to include the tragic fate of General Ross's driver, then continued with James's surprise proposal and how he'd seemed to be in such a rush. Then she finished her tale with when she'd overheard General Ross telling James to "get her out of the office."

"Wait. He was marrying you because he was following orders?" Reynolds asked, his beer held out in front of his face in mid-drink.

Susan nodded.

"Wow. I am so sorry. I knew Brogan was a little peculiar, but that's unbelievable. Thank goodness you found out now and not afterward."

The waitress arrived with their food then, and Susan realized it had taken her a half hour to tell her story.

"This is excellent," she said as she ate her shepherd's pie.

"It always is. This place is a little rough, but the cook is a treasure." The captain paused to take a sip of beer. "So you decided to investigate Ben Johnson's disappearance while you figure out what's next for you?"

"Yes, pretty much. I kept reading stories about all those poor people disappearing in the city and realized that I had my own unsolved mystery right in front of me. Ben left for Washington a few days after the explosion at Coney Island and just . . . disappeared. How does that happen?"

"That's not a bad question. It would be a lot easier for you to find answers if you still worked at Edison, though."

"Maybe. Maybe not. The general and James are too preoccupied with the radios while the trail goes cold, and I'm just a secretary. No one wants to talk to me. That explosion could have killed me, but I haven't been able to find out anything about it."

"You might be a secretary on paper, but I saw firsthand how valuable you were to Edison," said the captain between bites of shepherd's pie. "You led us right to that transmitter in the city."

"Thank you."

"But I'm afraid that, while you might not have underestimated your capability to gather information, you've clearly overestimated mine. I might be able to find something out, but I might be shut down for asking too many questions."

"Anything you can do to help would be wonderful. I'm not sure where to start. I was thinking about reaching out to Senator Mather next. We've met socially a few times, so I'm sure I can think of a—"

"Well, I was hoping to catch you here, Captain, but I had no idea I'd hit the jackpot," a familiar voice interrupted.

Susan spun around and found herself facing Carl Urich. "Carl! You know the captain?" she asked. "Oh, of course you do. You covered the story about Coney Island and the radios."

"Yes, he covered that story," said the captain, sounding as if he'd found something unwelcome stuck to the bottom of his shoe. "He covered it so well because he snuck into my hospital room, dressed as an orderly."

"And I brought you some whiskey and decent food, too," Carl said.

"Bribery," Reynolds said with a hint of a smile.

"The cost of doing business," Carl said, smiling back. "You two appear to be nearly finished with your dinners. May I take a seat?"

Susan nodded, while Reynolds shrugged.

Carl grabbed a chair from an empty table nearby and made himself comfortable. "What brings you out here, Susan?" he asked. "

Edison business? I don't see James."

"I'm here on my own," Susan said, sounding harsher than she wanted to. It was only the second time today, but Susan was tired of men expecting James to be at her side—or, more accurately, for her to be at his.

"Uh, okay. Can I ask why?"

"Sorry. I didn't mean to snap. I'm looking for information about Ben Johnson's disappearance."

Carl's brow wrinkled, but he said nothing.

"And what are you here for, Mr. Urich?" Reynolds asked. "What state secrets can I share with you?"

"Depends on what you consider a state secret," Carl said. "I know we disagree on that. I'm reporting on the *Mauretania* at the moment. I'm wondering if you can tell me about any radio chatter the night it disappeared."

"The *Mauretania*? Isn't that ship presumed lost at this point? No, we heard about it the same way you did: in the papers. There's no story there. Ships go down. It's terrible, especially when it's an important craft like the *Mauretania*, but it happens."

"It is, but word is it was carrying secret cargo. I'm wondering if it really was an accident."

"You see conspiracies everywhere, don't you?" Reynolds asked.

"Says the officer who lost three men and was nearly killed by a conspiracy inside our own Security Police," Carl said.

"Fair point. But you say the ship was carrying weapons? It was on its way here. Who's smuggling weapons into the United States?"

"Canada, actually. And I didn't say *weapons*, but it's a reasonable assumption. People who need untraceable weapons? Organized crime? The Black Army? Someone we don't know about?"

Reynolds frowned but said nothing.

"But you're saying there's been no chatter about the *Mauretania*?" Carl continued. "That's not strange to you? The second-largest ship in the world disappears, and no one has anything to say on Planetary Warning?"

Reynolds's brow wrinkled for a moment.

"Was there radio traffic when the *Titanic* went down?" Susan asked.

The captain and Carl both looked at Susan like they'd forgotten she was there.

"It was another major civilian liner, right?" Susan said with a shrug. Her glass was empty. Did she want another beer? She'd need to head home soon. She was already going to have to deal with the curfew when she got to West Orange.

"It's a good question," Reynolds said, and Carl nodded vigorously. "But the marines weren't running the station in 1910."

"But there are records," Susan said, looking at Carl. "Edison will have them. I can—I mean, they could dig them up for you."

"They?" Carl asked, his mouth open in surprise.

"I left a few days ago. It's a long story." Susan hoped she wouldn't have to recount it again so soon.

"I see. Do you have something else lined up, if you don't mind me prying?"

"But that's your job, isn't it?" Reynolds said, grinning again.

"Yeah, but I don't work for free," Carl said, not missing a beat. That elicited a laugh from the marine. "But that takes us back to my question, Susan. Are you working?"

"No, not yet," Susan said with a rueful grin.

"Well, if you're willing to commute and you're considering the city, there's an opening at *The Spectator*."

Susan hadn't thought about looking for a new position just yet, but here was an opportunity—complete with a reference— dropping right into her lap. But at a newspaper? Was she ready for that?

She'd thought about becoming a reporter back when she was a kid, but not at a paper like *The Spectator*. It had a terrible reputation as being the worst example of yellow journalism in the New York Tri-State area. Not to mention Susan had daydreamed about having her byline on the front page before President Bryan's crackdown on the news. Before William Randolph Hearst had gone to prison. Before the SPs had shuttered the *Daily News*. Journalism was dangerous—and Carl had reminded her a couple of days ago that he couldn't report on everything he wanted to.

And a job in the city? Susan had tried to convince James to move there a few months ago. Was she willing to do that by herself now? Well, whatever she was going to do, she was going to do it alone, since she had no interest in rushing into another relationship.

"*The Spectator*?" she asked. "What would I be doing? I'm not a reporter."

"Well, there's no reason you couldn't be," Carl said. "But that's not what I'm talking about. We need someone to take over the morgue."

"Morgue? *The Spectator* has its own morgue?" Reynolds asked, his mouth agape. "Is that even legal?"

Carl laughed. "A newspaper morgue is where we store old stories, photos, and research, Captain."

Reynolds shook his head in disgust, but Susan perked up. Old stories? Research? She could get paid to manage old stories? File research material? "So I'd be like a librarian for the paper?" she asked.

"In a manner of speaking, yes. The woman who used to run it retired. From what I've seen of you, I think you would take to it."

"That's an interesting idea. I'll give it some thought."

Carl smiled. "I understand. Newspapers aren't a popular career at the moment."

"What do you mean?" Reynolds said with a raised eyebrow.

"Seriously? Think about how you welcomed me a few moments ago and joked about how it's my job to pry. President Bryan and his people have managed to make everyone think we're the villains."

"Sure. Papers like *The Spectator*, but not the real news," Reynolds said.

Susan blanched.

"The real news," Carl said, chuckling.

"What's the supposed to mean?" Reynolds said with an edge in his voice. " Are you mocking me?"

"Everything you read in your 'real news' is approved by the SPs, Captain. All of it. At least with *The Spectator*, we let the occasional unauthorized fact slip through. I was within days of uncovering what Sean Fleming was up to years before your shoot-out with him."

"And what happened?" Reynolds demanded. "Why didn't you?"

"National Security," Carl said, making quotes in the air with his fingers.

Reynolds's brow furrowed. He looked into his beer mug and gestured for the waitress.

"Anyway, here's my card, Susan," Carl added. "Give me a call if you're interested."

Susan took the card and read it before she put it in her purse. It bore a midtown address for the newspaper, along with Carl's name and a telephone number.

Working at a newspaper in New York City would be a huge step. But having access to *The Spectator's* files might help her learn more about Ben's disappearance.

And what else did she have to do?

CHAPTER 11

Headquarters for *The Spectator* was in a four-story building three blocks uptown from Terminal City and a few short blocks from the prestigious Yale Club, Biltmore Hotel, and Grand Central Palace. It was an interesting place for a newspaper with a reputation as a "rag" and a "scandal sheet," but that was New York City. The sacred and the profane could share a pretzel and a park bench.

Susan stopped at the substantial double doors of 40 East 52nd Street. A tiny brass plaque and the oily funk of newspaper ink announced that she was at the right place. Could she work here, though? Would they allow her to spend her day working as a researcher for a newspaper? Well, the only way to find out was to sit down for an interview. She squared her shoulders and pushed open the double doors.

Inside, the mahogany-paneled foyer was lined with paintings of landscapes and framed newspapers, but it lacked the usual chairs and benches for visitors. At one end, barring the way between the elevators and the front door, was an enormous desk, fashioned from the same mahogany as the paneling. Behind it sat a uniformed man.

"Can I help you?" the guard growled as he stood, revealing a gun holstered on his left hip. He was clearly more security guard than receptionist.

"I'm here about a job?" Susan said. The man in front of her was much more threatening than the guards she'd faced on Long Island a few days earlier. What kind of place was this? She'd promised herself she'd at least do an interview, and letting a hostile security guard scare her off would mean breaking that vow.

"Your purse," the guard said.

"Huh?"

"Gimme your purse. Need to search it."

Susan clutched the purse's strap on her left shoulder as she stepped toward the guard's desk. She didn't have anything compromising in her bag, but the idea of a strange—and rather frightening—man rifling through it wasn't attractive, either. "Why?" she murmured. "There's nothing important in here."

"Rules. You don't get in without being searched."

Susan sighed, took the bag off her shoulder, and handed it to the guard. He grabbed it from her and turned it upside down, dumping the contents onto his desk. Susan gasped, and the guard tried—but failed—to suppress a smirk. He sifted through the pile of house keys, hairbrushes, makeup, and other sundries.

"Fine," he said.

"Fine?" Susan asked.

"Fine. You can pick your stuff up."

Susan flushed as she took the purse and scooped her belongings back into it. Was she going to go through this every morning? She glanced back at the double doors and considered walking right back through them, but she didn't want to let this man win, either.

She finished packing her stuff and turned toward the elevator.

"Hold on," the guard said, leering at her. "I gotta search you now."

"What? No," Susan said. That was a bridge too far.

"You want to get in, you gotta be searched."

Susan took a deep breath, turned away from the guard, and raised her arms. But before he could touch her, the elevator door opened.

"Vincent, I wanted to remind you that we have a friend of Mr. Urich's coming in about the open position in the morgue today," said the man who stepped off the elevator, then stopped in front of Susan and the guard. The man was at least six feet, three inches tall. He wore a worn leather jacket over a clean white shirt as well as brown pants, a tweed flat cap, and a perfectly trimmed gray beard, placing him somewhere in his late fifties or early sixties. He took a step back when he saw Susan. "Oh. I didn't see you there. Are you Susan Wilson?" he asked.

"Yes, I am," Susan said, fighting back tears of frustration.

"What's going on here?" the man growled at Vincent.

"I was just . . ." Vincent started.

"You were just shaking her down. I'll be talking to Mr. Fratelli about this."

"But I—"

"No buts. I told you we had a guest coming, and I can see from her expression that you've been up to your games again." The older man turned to Susan, his face tinged red with anger. to Susan. "Come on, Miss Wilson. Mr. Bell is waiting upstairs for you, and I believe you could use a cup of tea."

Who was Mr. Bell? Before Susan could ask, the older man led her to the elevator and pressed a button for the second floor.

"I'm sorry about that," he said as the elevator door closed. "Our normal guy is out for the week, and I can only work with what the . . . uh, family sends me. I'll have a talk with them and make sure he's gone by the end of the day. Oh, sorry. Sam Dodds." He extended a hand toward Susan.

Susan shook his hand. His grip was firm, but not overpowering. Sam filled the elevator with the strong but not unpleasant aroma of expensive cigars and a cologne with notes of vanilla, rum, and woodsmoke. When he'd stepped off the elevator, he'd seemed intimidating, but now he reminded Susan of the grandfather she'd never met.

"I'm in charge of security for the paper," Sam added. "We might as well get this out of the way up front: Sometimes this work can be a little dangerous. But I can promise you it's never boring." He gave Susan a wink and a smile.

The elevator opened to a long, broad great room occupying most of the second floor, with doors on the far end leading to offices for editors and senior reporters. It had a wall facing Park Avenue with tall windows that let in a generous amount of light for the four rows of desks running the long way across the room. On the opposite wall were posters, storyboards, and a few framed front pages. The newsroom buzzed with the sound of dozens of conversations, punctuated with the *clack-clack-clack* of typewriters and *tap-tap-tap* of feet as people ran up and down the aisles between the desks.

It was, in short, a mob scene. An atmosphere more suited for Coney Island or a dance hall, not an office.

"Welcome to the newsroom," Sam said as he reached into his jacket and pulled out a cigar, revealing a pistol secured in a shoulder holster on his left side. He lit the cigar and gestured for Susan to follow him toward the offices.

Susan followed him across the center of the room, shifting right and left to avoid collisions with men, women, and children hustling to and fro between the desks. Some excused themselves; others bulled right through. Most avoided any sort of contact at all.

When Susan and Sam reached the far end of the room, Sam walked over to a desk where a smartly dressed older woman was sitting. "This is Susan Wilson," Sam told her. "I think she needs a cup of chamomile tea." He gestured to Susan for acknowledgment.

Susan nodded.

"Pleased to meet you, Miss Wilson!" the woman said, offering Susan her hand. "I'm Joan."

Susan took it and introduced herself.

"Go ahead, Sam," Joan said. "They're waiting for you. And I'll fetch you that tea, Susan. Milk and sugar?"

"Black is fine," Susan said. She wasn't used to being served, but refusing the offer would have been ungrateful.

The office was larger than Susan had anticipated, as sizable as one of the larger laboratories back at Edison. Like the entrance foyer, it boasted rich mahogany panels, but these were decorated with portraits of men. Some sat alone; others posed with families. But they all looked visibly related to the man sitting behind a desk that matched the paneling perfectly. Carl Urich was sitting in front of the desk, but both men stood as Susan entered the room.

"There she is!" said the man behind the desk. "The girl of the hour." He was in his early thirties and clad in shirtsleeves, but the shirt appeared to have cost more than Sam's entire wardrobe. It was also accented with a silk tie that would have covered Susan's board at Mrs. Prendick's for half a year. He stood and offered Susan his hand.

"Jasper Bell," he said with an endearing grin. "I run this circus. Carl has told me a lot about you."

"All of it good, I promise," Carl said.

Susan shook Jasper's hand, then Carl's. Jasper gestured for her to take the chair next to Carl.

"If you don't need me here, sir, I need to take care of a situation with our substitute door guard," Sam said.

"Of course, Sam," Jasper said. "Thank you."

Sam left, closing the door behind him.

Jasper sat and rested his elbows on his massive desk. "I don't want to take up a lot of your time, Susan, but I like to meet all our prospective employees. Carl here tells me you were a valuable member of Edison's radio operation, but you're looking for new opportunities."

"Yes, that's right, sir," Susan said. It sounded like Carl hadn't divulged the details of why she had left Edison. She would have to thank him later, regardless of how things went.

"Please, call me Jasper. Mr. Bell is my father. He runs coal mines in Pennsylvania and thinks I should shut this rag down and come home." Jasper gave another of his smiles, and Susan wondered whether he was popular at the country club or wherever wealthy coal heirs met women. "So you were involved in the business with the Planetary Warning System in January?"

"Yes, I was," Susan said. Was this the only reason they wanted to talk to her? Were they hoping she'd tell them something she shouldn't? She shifted in her seat.

"And you were caught in the explosion at Edison, too, right?"

"Yes," Susan said. Was Jasper interviewing her for a job? Or for a story?

"That must have been something else. Terrifying, having a bomb go off at your office."

"Yes, it was," Susan said evenly.

"Is that why you're leaving Edison? The danger?"

"Huh? No, not at all. Like Mr. Urich said, I'm looking for new opportunities. I'm quite interested in the . . . morgue, as he called it? I'd like to see the kind of research that goes into stories and have a chance to look at older ones. I wouldn't mind getting involved in researching new stories."

"Great. That's what I wanted to hear. I wouldn't want you to come to *The Spectator* because of the danger at Edison. I don't want to frighten you, but the Security Police has it out for the press, and they'll pounce at any sign of disobedience. Also, the president's rhetoric has made us targets for some extremists, too."

A soft rap sounded on the door, and Joan slipped into the room with a teacup. She handed it to Susan wordlessly and left, closing the door behind her.

"Yes, Carl mentioned that to me," Susan said with a nod. She took a sip of the tea. Chamomile, like Sam Dodds had said.

"I'm not convinced your work for Edison is related to what

we need in the morgue," Jasper said. "But to be honest, a reference from Carl is all I need. You still live in New Jersey?"

"Yes, but I'm considering moving to the city," Susan said. "I don't have much left over there. I would want to make sure I'm going to fit in here, though." Which was true. She'd done some soul-searching the past few days, and unless she was interested in waitressing, cutting hair, or starting over in a field like nursing, West Orange didn't have much to offer her. And it would be easier to travel back to New Jersey to see her friends on weekends than to travel to the city every day for a job. But moving to the city would be consequential. She didn't want to do that and end up alone without a job.

"That makes sense. I'm aware of *The Spectator*'s reputation, and I understand why you might be intimidated, especially after what I said about the Security Police. But our reputation is the price we pay for telling the truth. The government wants us to . . . What was that phrase you used yesterday, Carl?"

"Take dictation," Carl said.

"Yes, that's it. Take dictation. Like with those radios they're handing out." Jasper pointed behind where Carl and Susan were seated.

Susan turned and saw a radio for the national network. It was bulky, more substantial than the initial plans James had drawn up when he'd been given the project. He'd come up with a bold design for the tuner; and Seward had said that while it was very clever, the fabrication would be too difficult. It seemed Seward had been right.

"When did that arrive?" Susan asked. She hadn't expected to see one for another few months.

"Last week," Carl said.

"It's a great reminder," Jasper said. "They want us to stay between the lines. Write about murder in soft words. We don't, so they're looking to replace us—or at least reduce our importance—with puppets. But either way, we have to be careful, even if our reporters sometimes forget that." He eyed Carl and gave him a wry smile. "But our mission is to tell the truth, even if it's unwelcome or uncomfortable."

Unwelcome was a word that suited *The Spectator*'s reputation well, in Susan's mind. Ben Johnson had been livid when Carl had shown up at the hospital while James was recovering from the injuries he'd received at Coney Island. And Siobhan, James's mother, still held a grudge from when Carl had tried to speak to James's father while he was dying from cancer. But in both cases, it turned out Carl had been onto something. He'd been on the verge of breaking stories about how Sean Fleming had been smuggling Martian hardware out of Edison and selling it.

Did this public interest extend to other stories? Or was *The Spectator* only interested in exposing corruption in the Security Police and the War Department?

"Like the story about the people disappearing from downtown?" Susan felt compelled to ask.

Jasper sat back in his chair, his brow wrinkled as he looked at Carl.

"Yes, stories like that," Carl said. "I've been looking at that one, and we've already printed a few articles about it."

"I'd like to visit the morgue, then," Susan said. "And meet the people I'd be working with."

"Oh, you'd be running the morgue on your own," Jasper said with a wide smile. "You'd be your own boss."

Susan's heart sped up. Her own boss? So she'd have complete access to the morgue. She'd be able to research what had happened to Ben, and she could talk to whoever was looking into the downtown disappearances, too.

"Carl will take you up to the morgue and show you what we're looking for," Jasper said. "If you like what you see, Joan can handle the details on salary and start date."

CHAPTER 12

"'m just saying it's weird, Phil," said Mildred, one of the older reporters on *The Spectator*'s staff. "The Martians surfaced in Europe more than six months ago, and we're over here, fighting over morals clauses in school charters. Are we ready for an attack? Why isn't anyone worried? Has everyone forgotten what the Martians did to us?"

"The navy is watching our coasts, and we have the Planetary Warning System," Phil said. "They're not going to sneak up on us, Mildred. And I do think some people are worried, but what can they do? Run to Kansas and hide in a cornfield?"

"I don't know what we're supposed to do. That's the point, Phil." Mildred stopped a few feet short of Susan's counter in the morgue and held out her hands. She was an inspiration to the other women at *The Spectator*. Susan might have missed out on being the first woman with a byline in the paper, but it didn't mean she hadn't caught herself daydreaming about following in Mildred's footsteps since she'd started working at the paper last week.

"Bryan got himself elected by promising to make sure we'd be safe," Mildred continued. "Hell, I voted for him the first time.

But what do we have now? A federal police force? Weekly worship services in schools? Newspaper owners in prison?"

"I'm no fan of his, either," Phil said. "You're already aware of that. I'm just saying we're not sitting ducks for a Martian attack."

Mildred and Phil had come to the morgue to pick up research for their stories. Phil, who handled the crime beat for the Bronx, had requested all the stories about pickpockets in his borough from 1905 to 1912. Mildred was looking for background on Tammany Hall's activity in Brooklyn after the first Martian Attack. Now, Susan set aside the files she'd pulled on Edison and Ben Johnson and picked up their papers. It had only been a week since she'd accepted the job offer at *The Spectator*, but she was having the time of her life. Was it a honeymoon period? Or would this last? She didn't care; she was going with it.

"Here you go," Susan said, handing each reporter their files.

"What do you think, Susan?" Mildred asked. "Are we ready for an attack?"

"Actually, I heard you were caught in some action already this year, right?" Phil interjected. "The mess with the radio towers?"

"Um, yes. I was," Susan said. "The Planetary Warning System is back up, but that's all I can say."

Phil grinned. "All you know? Or all you can say?"

A little of both, really. After the team at Edison had restored the radios, they'd been in contact with a group of German soldiers who claimed to have a way to disable Martian weapons, including their Tripods—the deadly walking machines—and heat rays. James had initially been tagged to build a Tripod based on the Martians' plans, but the War Department had redirected him to the National Radio Network and, presumably, handed it off to someone else.

But Susan wasn't sure she could talk about that—and she didn't want to, anyway. She was here to work in the morgue, not act as a source for stories about Edison and the War Department. "All I know," she said. "I think you have a point about the navy covering the coasts, and the army is still holding the border with Mexico. And the National Radio Network is supposed to act as an early warning system when it's operational."

Mildred snorted. "So we get word on when to run and hide?"

Susan shrugged, and watched as the reporters took their files over to the long tables set up for research at the far end of the room. Mildred was right, of course. The radio network was a distraction at best, and the propaganda Carl called it at worst. But what could Susan do? Give the reporters a story that could get them all locked up? Or go back to Edison and force James to do something?

He was back from his trip west and had knocked on Mrs. Prendick's front door, looking for Susan. Fortunately, Susan had still been on the train home from the city, and Maggie had taken care of James. "Trust me, he won't be back," she'd said. Susan hoped that would be the case, but she was still looking for a place to stay in the city. She'd already spoken to the woman responsible for *The Spectator*'s classified section and asked her to keep her apprised of promising listings. So far, she'd provided Susan with two places to check out.

The elevator door opened again. Sam Dodds stepped off with a crumbled piece of paper in one hand.

"Did you drop this downstairs, Susan?" he asked. "I found it under the guard's desk. Maybe it fell when that thug shook you down on your first visit?" He handed her the flyer announcing the weekly meetings at the church downtown.

"Why, yes, it is," Susan said. "Thank you for asking instead of throwing it away."

"It's for those people who've been disappearing, huh?" Sam said, looking at the flyer over her shoulder. "The next meeting is tonight."

"It is. I ran into a man who's lost his cousin."

"Damn shame. All those people, and nothing anyone can do about it." Sam shook his head.

"Nothing?" Susan asked. What could he possibly mean? Of course there was something someone could do about it.

"People don't want to be found, you can't find 'em."

"You think hundreds of people all decided to disappear in the past few weeks?"

"What else could it be? Disappearing that many people would take some serious resources."

Susan looked at the flyer again. Yes, it would take serious resources to do that. Someone was behind these disappearances, and someone else needed to do something about it. Those apartments would have to wait.

CHAPTER 13

Redeemer Baptist Church was a storefront on a narrow side street. It sat between a tattoo parlor and a shuttered warehouse, and across the street from a taxi stable. Susan didn't have any problems finding the church, though, because a line extending out the door and all the way to the avenue led her right to it.

It was nearly six o'clock. Would Susan make it into the church before nightfall? She'd been cutting it close with the curfew too often lately. But if she was going to do something to help with these disappearances, even if it was as simple as uncovering information for Carl, this was the time and place to start.

The line was a survey of New York City's poor communities, with a variety of ages, skin colors, styles of dress, and family situations. But one detail was immediately obvious: they were all members of the city's working class. None of the men wore suits. All the women were dressed for working in factories or raising children and keeping homes.

The line crawled for a few minutes, then stopped. Eventually, the familiar face of the young man who had handed Susan the flyer approached, carrying a clipboard. He stopped at each group in line, spoke to them for a few moments, wrote some notes, and moved on.

"Hello. Who are you missing, ma'am?" he asked when he reached Susan. His pencil was poised over the clipboard, and fatigue—likely both emotional and physical—showed in his eyes.

"No one," Susan said, seeing no recognition in his eyes. "We met a couple of weeks ago? You gave me this flyer."

The young man looked up from his notes and made eye contact with Susan. Finally, after an uncomfortable pause, recognition dawned. "Oh! In the Village!" he said with a tired smile. "The day that guy gave me a hard time. I'm glad you made it."

"You're gathering names? That's not a bad idea. It might help the police."

"The police? No, they wouldn't do anything with this. I'm gathering names—at least from the people who aren't afraid— and addresses to see if there's some kind of pattern. Maybe if I can find one, I can create some interest in this."

"*The Spectator* had a reporter looking at this," Susan said. "I think he might have hit a dead end, though." That wasn't entirely true, but she didn't want to explain how Carl had been distracted by the *Mauretania*.

"I didn't know that. Do you work for the paper, Miss . . ."

"Wilson. Susan Wilson. Actually, I started there recently. After we met, Mr. . . ."

"Oh, sorry. Steven. Steven Williams. So you're a reporter?"

"No. I work in, uh, research at the paper. But I'm hoping I can find something that might help the reporter who's covering the story. I hope that's okay with you."

"Anything." Steven glanced back at the line. "I need to talk to the rest of the families. Do you want to wait inside? I can tell them to let you into the church."

"Can I come with you?" Susan offered. "It might help me if I hear what the folks have to say."

•   •   •

Over the next hour, Susan and Steven spoke to crying mothers, angry fathers, and devastated brothers, sisters, and cousins. They wanted answers. They all needed a sign that someone cared, that someone was looking for their loved ones, even if no one was there to help them.

Later, Susan slumped into a chair in the storefront church and accepted a cup of tepid coffee from Steven. The only patterns in what she'd learned from the people she'd met were what she already knew: the missing people were all poor and from south and east of the site of the Tesla fire.

She set the coffee down and put her head in her hands. What to do? And where to start? She'd lost her parents during the first Martian Attack when she'd been young, and it had hurt. But so had half the kids in her school. It was a sudden, universal event that had touched everyone, one way or another. These disappearances, however, were a slow burn: one person at Battery Park, two more in the eastern reaches of Greenwich Village. It wasn't an event that touched everyone, so most people didn't notice or care.

"Are you all right, young lady?" asked a deep voice Susan hadn't heard before.

She lifted her head and turned in the direction the question had come from. An older Black couple stood behind her, with expressions of genuine concern on their faces.

"Yes, thank you," Susan said. "Just tired and a little drained."

"We saw you helping Steven talk to the families," the man said, "but we've never seen you in the church."

"Oh, I'm not a member here," Susan said. "I met Steven when he was handing out flyers and came to see how I could help. You've lost someone, too?"

"Lisa, our daughter," the man said.

"I'm very sorry," Susan said. The pain visible in both the man's eyes and his wife's made her chest ache. She stood and offered her hand to the man. "My name is Susan. I wish we were meeting under different circumstances."

"I'm Anthony, and this is my wife, Audrey," the man said.

"She was a good girl, our Lisa," Audrey said. "She was working in a bank and taking night courses for typing and shorthand."

"I work on the East Side docks, and my wife worked in the Garment District until her hands gave out," Anthony explained. "We were so proud to watch our daughter use her head as much as her hands."

"You must be proud," Susan said.

Anthony smiled. "Yes, we are. It's not easy for people like us to work our way out of the factories and the docks, even up here in the North. My father was a freed man and fled here in the '80s. He would have been so proud of his granddaughter working at a bank."

"I'm sure he would. It sounds like you raised a wonderful girl."

"Sorry about that, Susan," Steven said as he approached the group. "I needed to introduce Pastor Nelson to someone. But I see you've met the Watts family."

"Yes, Lisa sounds like a wonderful daughter," Susan said. "But I need to head back to New Jersey so I don't run afoul of the curfew."

"You came here from Jersey?" Anthony asked.

"I work in the city, and I'm looking for a place over here. But for now, I have to commute."

"Susan works for *The Spectator*," Steven said. "She's going to try to get the paper to cover this story."

Anthony's eyes lit up. "Really? You will?"

"I'm going to try. But I'm a researcher. I can't make any promises, Mr. Watts," Susan said, not wanting to set Anthony and Audrey up for disappointment. But she was going to do everything she could to make sure everyone knew about these missing people.

"Thank you, Susan," Anthony said, wiping away a tear. "Thank you."

CHAPTER 14

Minutes later, Susan hustled around the corner to Grand Street and headed west. It was only a little after eight, so she had plenty of time to get out of the city before curfew. But there was no reason to risk getting in trouble because of a missed or late train.

"So what did you learn?" asked a familiar voice as Susan hustled down Grand toward the West Side and the train under the Hudson. She stopped to see Sam Dodds behind her, hurrying to catch up.

"Learn?" Susan said. "I'm not sure what you mean, Mr. Dodds." Based on his question, this was no chance meeting. He was following her. She suppressed a shiver.

"I'm assuming you're here because of the flyer I returned to you this afternoon," he said. "I don't think you're missing any family members, so I'm guessing you were looking into the story."

"Well, uh, not much." Susan checked her watch. "I need to catch the train, Mr. Dodds. Can we walk and talk?"

"Of course. I spoke to Carl, and he said he didn't put you on this. So you're investigating the disappearances on your own?"

So Sam had spoken to Carl? Were they talking about what

she was doing in her free time? Susan had left Edison because of men who wanted to decide where and when she should be. Was she ever going to get away from it?

"I might be," Susan said, struggling to keep her voice level as she hurried down the street and managed her temper. "I'm not sure why you and Mr. Urich would be interested in that?"

"I'm merely trying to make sure you're safe, Susan. This is downtown New York City, not the sleepy streets of New Jersey." Was that concern on Sam's face? Or was he being patronizing?

"I'm fine, Mr. Dodds. I had more trouble getting into *The Spectator* for my interview than I did at Redeemer Baptist Church."

Sam inhaled sharply. Whether it was in shock or anger, Susan couldn't tell. But by then, they'd reached the Bowery, where they had to stop for traffic. Susan crossed her arms and tapped her foot while horse-drawn carts and gasoline-powered cars and trucks sped up and down the avenue. A heavyset police officer, wielding a whistle and standing next to a post with signs on top, directed traffic from the center of the intersection of Grand and Bowery. The sign rotated so that "Stop" or "Go" faced the proper direction, depending on which way he wanted traffic to go. And at that moment, a man piloting a cart full of apples clearly wanted the officer to rotate his sign.

"C'mon, it's been five minutes a'ready!" the cart driver heckled.

The officer either didn't hear him or didn't care. Another minute passed.

"Goddammit!" the cart driver shouted. "It's time to go!"

"If you don't watch your mouth, you'll be headed to the Tombs instead of back to your garage!" the officer shouted.

The cart driver muttered an obscenity, which Susan over-heard. Another sixty seconds passed.

"Fer Chrissakes, come on!" the cart driver bellowed.

Sam tilted his head to catch Susan's eye and grinned. So did Susan, in spite of herself.

"I'm gonna lock you up!" the police officer shouted back.

The cart driver muttered a more colorful obscenity and hied his horse. It bolted across the avenue, narrowly missing the cart that was crossing Grand. Traffic stopped in all directions as the apple cart peeled down Grand with the police officer in pursuit.

Susan looked both ways before dashing across Bowery. She heard Sam's footfalls closely behind her.

"Wasn't Edison working on a new traffic signal based on radio technology?" Sam asked when they reached the other side of the street and continued at their previous pace.

"Edison Laboratories was," Susan said. "Or is, I suppose. But that's in Princeton, not where I worked." James had consulted on the project once. The idea had been to use radio signals to sense how busy traffic was in each direction and bias the signal toward reducing congestion. But while the radio waves had done a decent job at sensing faster-moving vehicles, they'd proven unreliable at picking up pedestrians and slow carts.

"I can see you're upset with me, Su—I mean, Miss Wilson," Sam said.

"Can you?" Susan asked.

"I just want to be sure you're safe—"

"I assure you, Mr. Dodds, I'm fine. I've been on my own for years, and I know how to navigate the city, despite being raised in the 'sleepy streets of New Jersey.' I don't need a couple of men deciding where I should or should not go." At that point, Susan realized she'd stopped in the middle of the sidewalk and was drawing stares.

"Two men . . . deciding? You think Carl sent me after you?" Sam asked.

Susan reached Broadway and waited for a signal from one of the two police officers directing traffic there. "Are you headed to the west side?" she asked.

"I'm headed to the tubes. Aren't you?"

"Are you following me to the sleepy streets, Mr. Dodds?" Susan was almost afraid of the answer.

"I live in Jersey City."

Susan raised an eyebrow as she crossed the street. Sam held his hands out and shrugged.

"Carl didn't send you after me?" she asked.

"No. I only asked him if he had you investigating the story. He said no because he'd reached a dead end and wasn't looking into it at all. He's tied up with something he calls power supplies and the *Lusitania*."

"*Mauretania*," Susan corrected. What power supplies was Sam—or, rather, Carl—talking about? Did he mean the Martian ones? Like the one Tesla had wreaked all that havoc with?

"Whatever. He said the church, and the story, would be a dead end."

"Well, he's wrong."

"Oh? About what? The church? Or the story?"

"Both."

"Really?" Sam asked as a train pulled into the station.

"I spoke to at least a hundred people who care about those disappearances," Susan said.

"That's fair," Sam said. "But we're a newspaper, not the police or private investigators."

"The police aren't doing anything. Isn't it our job to change that? To make our readers care so there's pressure for the police to act?"

"Act on what? Maybe these people don't want to be found."

"Don't want to be found? So hundreds of sons, daughters, wives, and husbands just up and left their lives for greener pastures?"

"Maybe. It's a big, crowded city. Who's to say they didn't decide to go somewhere else? They could be ten blocks away, and their families might never find them."

Susan shook her head. Sam didn't understand. He hadn't spoken to the people she had. Hadn't looked them in the eye and listened to their stories. But Susan was too tired to argue. She shook her head and kept walking.

"But you're still going to follow this, aren't you?" Sam asked. Susan nodded.

"Of course," Sam said. "So I'm going to have to train another reporter."

Susan spun around to face him. "Train? What do you mean?"

"You don't think my only job is managing the reception desk and returning lost paperwork, do you?" Sam's smile didn't quite reach his eyes. "I'm in charge of security, Miss Wilson. That includes the security of our reporters in and out of the office."

Susan's heart sped up. She wanted to help those people, but did that mean she needed training? To protect herself? The image of the gun Sam carried in his jacket surfaced in her mind. "What kind of training?" she asked. "Will I need to carry a gun?"

"No! At least not yet. You won't be walking into the kind of danger Carl or Phil are." Sam tilted his head toward Susan. "At least you better not."

"Carl has a gun? And Phil, too?"

"This is Bryan's America, Miss Wilson. Any smart man is carrying a weapon."

CHAPTER 15

"Damn," Susan said out loud, startling herself with her own profanity. Clearly, she'd been spending too much time training with Sam Dodds over the past couple of weeks. She absentmindedly rubbed her right shoulder, which was still a little sore from her last "lesson."

When she hadn't been participating in "safety" training with Sam, she'd been researching the names of the missing in *The Spectator*'s archives. So far, one hundred fifteen names out of more than two hundred twenty people had turned up exactly nothing. Susan had said it would be a wild goose chase when Carl told her to check them, and so far she'd been right.

After her first visit to Redeemer Baptist Church, Susan had gone to Carl the next day and tried to reinforce the importance of the story of the missing people. Carl hadn't disagreed, but he'd insisted the story of the *Mauretania* and the missing Martian—yes, Martian—power supplies was more important. But Susan could do something, he'd said. He'd called it the "legwork" and insisted it wasn't an off-color term. What he'd meant was, Susan could take the list of names she'd helped Steven gather and research them in the archives in between anything she needed to rummage through for the other reporters.

It had taken her a week to retrieve a copy of the list, and she'd had to attend services at Redeemer to do it. It turned out Steven spent his days working a delivery cart for a bakery in Brooklyn when he wasn't handing out flyers in different neighborhoods. Since then, Susan had been checking names against the paper's files—a tall order, since the morgue lacked any kind of central indexing system. There was a reason it was the "morgue" and not the "library."

To Susan, the entire project felt like a distraction. A way to get her out of Carl's hair. But if she was going to convince him to help, she would do what he'd asked.

She had just picked up the arrest records from Midtown's Seventh Precinct and started scanning for the next name when the elevator buzzed and the door slid open.

"Hey, I heard you found a place while I was away," said Mildred as she stepped off the elevator.

Susan looked up from the list. "Yes! I did. I'm already moved in and enjoying the shorter ride to work."

"So where are you?" Mildred asked.

"Twenty-Third and Seventh," Susan said with a smile.

"Ooh, that's a wonderful neighborhood. You have the perfect pub around the corner, and Macy's is just a few blocks away. You're going to have to invite me over," Mildred said with a laugh.

"Absolutely!" Susan said and smiled back. She wasn't going to pass up a chance to make a new friend in her new hometown. "So how was the wedding?"

"Fun!" Mildred said. "Beautiful service, great people. I wish I could travel back to Chicago more often. We should go for lunch so I can tell you the whole story. Jake said you gathered some historical tax records for him?"

"Ah, yes. The Bronx. Here you go." Susan picked up a folder and handed it to Mildred.

As Mildred accepted the folder, the elevator buzzed again.

"Oh! I gotta catch that," Mildred said. "Bye, Susan. Good

morning, Carl!" She jogged over, nearly knocking Carl Urich over as he stepped out of the elevator.

"Hi Carl," Susan said.

"Good morning," Carl said. "Any luck?"

"Of course not," Susan snapped, regretting the outburst as soon as it left her lips.

"Of course not?"

"Sorry. Just frustrated."

"You think I'm wasting your time?" Carl asked.

"No, it's just that . . . well, yes, actually." Had more of Sam Dodd's bluntness rubbed off on Susan than she'd guessed?

"I guess I can see why you might feel that way," Carl said.

Susan gasped. So he *had* been wasting her time? Was he confessing?

"Reporting isn't just waiting for disgruntled radio engineers to bring you information about conspiracies in cafés," Carl continued. "In fact, it almost never is. It's tedium. Legwork. Pounding the pavement."

Perfect. Another lecture. Susan crossed her arms.

"How do you think I found James?" Carl asked.

"What do you mean?" Susan asked.

"I approached James last year, after the incident at Coney Island. How do you think I found him?"

"You met him at the hospital," Susan said. "He was on his way home with Ben Johnson." James had been upset at the time, because he'd felt Ben had been pressuring him to go to work after waking up in the hospital. Carl's questions about the incident and Ben's reaction to them hadn't helped; they'd made James even more suspicious.

"I saw him there, yes," Carl said. "But Johnson got him out of there before I could catch his name. So I spent the rest of that day —and a good chunk of the evening—up here in the morgue, going through local newspapers before I found a story about a promising young man who'd won a science fair. I missed that he had an even closer connection to the story, but I caught on to that later."

Susan uncrossed her arms.

"That's reporting," Carl said. "Or at least a big part of it. Now, what do you know about these missing people?"

"Nothing! That's the problem."

"No, you know quite a bit. You can tell me where they're from. You've seen what they have in common, at least some of what they share. Tell me."

"Well, they're from the city," Susan started.

"They're not only from the city," Carl said. "C'mon, Susan. You told me more than this about them before you got the list. Where are they from?"

Susan crinkled her brow in concentration. "They're from downtown."

"Exactly. And?" Carl smiled and made a gesture like he was ushering Susan through a door.

"I don't know anything else, Carl. I can't find many records at all, not even from the census President Bryan ran a couple of years ago. They're all laborers of one kind or another, or the children of laborers. From families who emigrated from Europe or fled the South after the War of the Rebellion. Many of them are the children or grandchildren of freed slaves." Susan began stroking her chin then.

"So if I wanted to abduct someone without a trace, they'd be the ideal candidates?" Carl asked.

"Well, yes," Susan said. What was Carl trying to say? The fact that a mystery existed was part of the solution?

"They're nobodies," Carl said.

Susan frowned, then opened her mouth to argue.

"Not the term I'd use," Carl said, holding up a hand to suppress Susan's objection. "But it's what the police—or, to be honest, most people—would call them. Trying to find out who they are is not going to help. The next step might be to look into where they disappeared from."

So he *did* think there was a story. "How do I do that?" Susan asked.

"Go back to the families. Ask them. Was it on their way to work? On their way home? To or from school? Do these kids go to school? Or do they work, too? Did a bunch of them work at the same places, and they all disappeared in the same area or near the same train?"

"So you think this is worth looking into," Susan said. "Will you help me, then?"

Carl shook his head. "I can't. I have a bigger story."

"Bigger than hundreds of missing people?"

"I think so. What I'm following might be another Tesla fire in the making."

"You're still looking into the *Mauretania*? You think it was carrying Martian hardware? Missing power supplies?"

"Yes, for the Canadians. The *Mauretania* was scheduled to stop at Halifax, which wasn't part of her normal route."

"But it sank. That stuff's at the bottom of the Atlantic now," Susan said with a shrug.

"And I think someone wanted it there," Carl said. "I'm headed out to Washington to talk to a few shipping contacts."

Susan winced. The last time she'd heard someone say they were headed to Washington, DC, that person had been Ben Johnson. She'd never seen him again. "Be careful," she said.

"How about you? You've been working with Sam?" Carl asked.

"Yes. We've covered observation and some basic self-defense." Susan rubbed her right shoulder. "Does everyone go through all this with him?"

"No, it's optional. But if you're smart, you'll finish it." Carl turned to head toward the elevator as he added, "You don't survive Little Bighorn without learning a few things."

Susan gawked. "Little Bighorn?"

"Yep. Whatever you do, don't mention Custer around Sam. Hates the man."

CHAPTER 16

Mildred had been right about Susan's new place, but she only knew half the story. The apartment was in a spectacular neighborhood, with a nice grocer, a great pub, and Macy's biggest store a short walk away. But it was also on the fifth floor in a building with no elevator.

"It'll keep you young!" the landlord had quipped. Susan had laughed at the time, still head over heels at finding a place she could afford in a safe place close to work. She hadn't yet realized that what he'd meant was, "It'll kill you before you can get old." Still, it was her own place with a private bathroom (something Susan hadn't had since living with her aunt), a sizable bedroom, and radiators she could control when it got cold.

She reached the third-floor landing and stopped for a moment to rest her tired back and legs. Susan had spent the last three evenings interviewing families and friends of missing people and wanted nothing more than an aspirin, a cup of tea, and her soft bed.

Once she got to the fifth floor, she unlocked her door, walked in, kicked off her heels, and started the kettle. Whatever pattern Carl thought she'd uncover by going back to the families had eluded her so far. All the missing people had simply disappeared without a trace. No notes. No signs. No trails. They were "nobodies," as Carl had put it. They had no traces to leave. One day, they were there; the next, they weren't. A few had worked in the same places, which made sense. But a few others worked in Brooklyn, and one even worked in the pencil factory in Jersey City.

It was as if someone was traveling around the city after dark, scooping people off the streets and secreting them away.

The kettle boiled. Susan poured the hot water into her mug, added some sugar, and sat at her tiny kitchen table. A hot bath sounded glorious, even if it was a little warm outside. Her feet and back would appreciate it. But first, the tea.

Susan had considered stalking the streets herself more than a few times already this week. But that would be absurd. Sam Dodds had shown her a few ways to defend herself, but she wasn't ready to face whoever had managed to kidnap hundreds of men, women, and children.

Speaking of which, she'd forgotten to lock her door and leave the key in the slot the way Sam had shown her. She dragged herself to her feet, grabbed her keys, and walked over to secure the apartment. She was on her way back to the kitchen table when she slipped and fell to one knee.

"What the hell!" Susan said. Sam's influence again. Damn him. She giggled as she stood and spotted the culprit. Someone had slid a note under her door. Another flyer? All the way up on the fifth floor? That was a dedication.

Susan picked it up and found it was an envelope. She tore it open and pulled out a single piece of carefully folded paper that read: *Get to pier 55 by 1 tomorrow nite. See the real story.*

She stumbled back, barely making it into the kitchen chair and knocking her tea onto the floor. Someone was watching her? Following her? They knew what she was investigating and where she lived?

She read the note again: *Get to pier 55 by 1 tomorrow nite.* That meant one o'clock in the morning. But at a pier? Was this a trap?

Or was someone feeding Susan information because they had something to hide? And where was Pier 55? She'd need to check in the morgue. They had to have maps with the piers on them.

Did that mean Susan had already decided she was going? Of course it did. She didn't have any choice, did she?

CHAPTER 17

I t was warm the following night. Too warm for the bulky coat and baggy pants Susan had picked up at the consignment shop. "For my father," she'd told the nun at the 12th Street mission, remembering a lesson from Sam about bad liars saying too much, instead of quitting while they were ahead.

Susan didn't like lying. Not after uprooting her entire life because of James's lack of honesty, and especially not to a nun. But she needed a safe way to travel through one of the city's most dangerous neighborhoods alone and after curfew. A man wearing a coat and hat in early summer would attract less attention than a terrified young lady hiking the East Side in sensible shoes.

Of course, Susan knew she didn't have to do it alone. She could have told Sam Dodds about the anonymous note. So why didn't she?

Because he'd tell her it was a trap, or he'd insist on going instead, leaving her safe at home.

Because she needed to prove she was capable of seeing it through herself.

And, most importantly, because she had promised Anthony and Audrey Watts that she would help them find their daughter.

If Carl Urich was too busy chasing after sunken luxury cruisers, she'd have to do it on her own. So Susan would uncover whatever was going on at Pier 55, whether it was an elaborate trap or a clue that would help her learn where Lisa and all the other missing people had gone.

Broome Street was reassuringly quiet as Susan walked past shuttered warehouses. Gas lamps illuminated the street corners, leaving yawning gaps of darkness in each block. Grand Street would have taken her right to the pier, but it would have been crowded, even after the curfew. The police had all but given up on the Lower East Side since the Tesla fire and the city's decision to abandon the East River Bridge project. One of the books in the morgue said the Bowery never sleeps, and that was still true all the way to the East River.

Susan had only been working in the city for a little over a month and had moved into her new apartment a little over a week ago. Now, she was wandering the streets at midnight, straying away from the tenements and shops she was only now starting to feel comfortable in and over to the East River, where industry ruled. Did that mean she had the makings of a reporter? Or had she simply lost her mind?

Based on the maps Susan had found in the morgue, an abandoned factory building sat on the far side of East Street from Pier 55. She had about thirty minutes to walk to it, get inside, and find a vantage point where she could learn who was taking people out of the city.

A pair of men turned onto Grand at Columbia Street and walked west, straight toward Susan. She gripped the leather case with the field glasses she'd purchased from a pawn shop near the mission. She hadn't needed a story to get those; the man behind the counter had been too busy hiding his smutty magazine to hear anything she would have tried to say.

Susan caught herself slowing her pace but sped back up to normal. She needed to think like a man. She had gotten here first, and she'd be damned before she gave any ground. So she reminded herself to move like a man. Straight ahead. Confident. Direct.

Reckless.

The two men stepped to one side to give Susan room as she walked by. One of them glanced sidelong at her, but Susan stayed on course, careful to avoid eye contact. Every nerve in her body wanted to check behind her and make sure the men were still walking west. She fought the urge, though, and won when she crossed Columbia Street.

Crisis averted.

Susan recalled the note one more time: *Get to pier 55 by 1 tomorrow nite. See the real story.* The real story. What had the note's author meant by that? Was Susan wasting her time? Was she about to watch a crew of moonshiners unloading illicit liquor from Long Island?

Or was she walking into a trap? Whoever had slipped the letter under her door could have just as easily waited and killed her, or had their way with her. She shivered at the thought.

She turned right at the corner of East and Broome Streets, putting the lesson she learned a few blocks earlier into practice: act as if you know where you're going. Stopping here, so close to her goal, would only attract attention.

As Susan walked south on East Street, her gaze drifted up to the roof of her destination. Someone was up there! Susan's heart leaped into her throat. It was a trap. Whoever had left the note must have been waiting for her.

She fought the urge to stop and gawk, maintaining her pace as she reached Grand Street and making a quick right turn. She had to keep walking, though she was ready to hyperventilate. The first turn was onto Tompkins Street. Susan took it and walked all the way back to Broome before she stopped.

She leaned against the wall, forcing her breathing to slow. She had to leave. She needed to go back home. But was she even safe in her own place? If so, then she'd need to go back to New

Jersey. Back to Mrs. Prendick. She'd beg for her old room if she had to. Maybe she'd have to go back to James. He'd help her—

Wait. How would the note's author know that Susan had gone to that specific warehouse? They weren't waiting for her. At least, not waiting for her to come right to them. So was the warehouse roof a lookout? Was someone watching for her? Or perhaps a guard was waiting for whatever was going to happen at the pier?

But Susan couldn't run. She had to see things through. Anthony and Audrey were counting on her. Lisa was counting on her.

She walked back to Broome and East, pulled the field glasses out of the voluminous overcoat, brought them up to her eyes, and directed them toward the pier. But she couldn't steady the glasses well enough to see anything. So she braced a forearm against the corner of the warehouse she was standing by and tried again.

Perfect. The light was poor, and the view was partially obscured, but Susan could make out the pier. She couldn't see much, but it was better than nothing. Examining the pier through the glasses, she sized up what appeared to be a fishing gear box that she could use as cover.

"Whatcha lookin' at, buddy?" said a voice from behind her.

Susan jumped, but managed to suppress a yelp that might have exposed her masquerade. "Nothing," she said, trying her best to lower her voice a few octaves. She broke out into a sweat as her heart raced. What if the source of the voice figured out she was a woman? Would he attack her? Raise a fuss? Was he an undercover SP? Or part of whoever was making people disappear?

If he was, it was an impressive disguise. This man hadn't seen a bed, bath, or barber in maybe a decade. He was small, shorter than Susan, but made up for it in bulk. Even under rumpled clothes and ages of dirt and grime, he looked like he worked for a living. Or at least he had before climbing into a bottle.

"Gotta drink?" he asked as he stumbled into Susan, pushing her back a few feet. He felt as heavy as he looked, and he launched Susan onto her rump in the middle of East Street.

"Nope," she said as she climbed to her feet. "I'm out."

"Hey, yer not too steady on yer feet," the man said as he wandered off to the west. "Mebbe you should lay off the sauce, buddy."

Susan heaved a sigh of relief as the man lumbered off. Had the encounter alerted anyone? Had he attracted unwanted attention?

She looked around for a moment. Apparently not. Just a couple of drunks by the river, if anyone had seen them at all. But where had he come from? She should have seen him, or at least heard him stumble along the street.

Susan doubled back and saw where he might have come from. A door leading into the warehouse was ajar! Had the man been inside?

She checked her watch. Twelve fifty. Enough time to check and see if there was a better vantage point inside.

Susan pulled the door open enough to squeeze through, pausing long enough to let her eyes adjust to the dark. She had walked into a gigantic room. Tall, broad windows lined the longer walls along the east and west sides of the warehouse, and the gas lamps on East Street cast enough light so that Susan could navigate without falling and breaking her neck. Large doors that were wide enough to fit three or four carts opened on the far end of the structure. Barrels lined the warehouse's walls. Beer, based on the sour tang that hung in the air.

A narrow wooden stairway stood to Susan's left. She climbed them, hoping she'd find a perch to observe the pier from. The stairs landed on a platform filled with more barrels, a hand truck, and a small desk directly under a window on the south-eastern corner of the warehouse. Perfect.

Susan cleaned the window as well as she could with the cuff of her coat. Then she pulled out her notepad and field glasses, and waited. But not for long.

A boat, maybe sixty feet long, pulled up to the pier and docked. Four men carrying rifles disembarked, established a perimeter around the pier, and waited.

Established a perimeter. Susan was thinking like a soldier now. Thanks, Sam Dodds.

But these men were dressed more like dockhands or farmers than like soldiers. They wore dungarees, flannel shirts, and canvas jackets. Were they veterans who had found work as private security? Smugglers?

Or was it a ruse? Now Susan was thinking like Carl.

Susan and the perimeter-establishing men waited for another ten minutes before two long covered wagons drove up to the pier. Six more men—three from each wagon—hopped out of the back of each one. Four established a perimeter of their own; and as soon as they were done, the others went to one of the wagons and led out their cargo.

Bile climbed into Susan's throat. Her hands ached as she clutched the field glasses in stark disbelief. It was people. The cargo was people in chains.

Men. Women. Maybe even a few boys in their teens. They were bound together by their hands and feet, so the group moved slowly and painfully from the back of the wagon and onto the pier, giving Susan enough time to examine each prisoner. Twenty-four people of varying ages and sexes—and every one of them looked tired, wretched, and filthy.

Susan scribbled down the count and a few descriptions. What was she watching? Kidnapping? Slavery?

One of the minders was having fun, pushing and shoving his victims as they shuffled down the pier. He cuffed one man on the back of the head, sending him—and all the people chained behind him—to the deck.

The group was climbing onto the boat when a man in a

heavy overcoat similar to the one Susan was wearing climbed out of one of the wagons. He was tall and lean, and something about the way he sauntered up to one of the perimeter guards seemed familiar to Susan.

She pulled the focus on the field glasses, but the man in the overcoat turned away as he spoke to the guard. What she could see, though, was the black pants and leather boots a man might wear with a Security Police uniform. She checked the footwear of the men guarding the carts. Three of them wore similar boots.

Were the SPs taking people in secret? She'd heard horror stories about them before, especially since she'd started working at *The Spectator*. But twenty-four at once? In chains, and in the middle of the night? Even Carl would have been shocked.

The man in the overcoat was standing under a gas lamp when he finally turned and exposed his face. Susan swung the field glasses over to him, but before her eyes focused on him, she already knew. Her heart raced, and her throat went dry as she realized who she was looking at.

It was Sean Fleming.

No. It couldn't be. He was a fugitive. He couldn't be operating right here in New York.

Susan watched as he spoke to one of the men from the boat and then turned in her direction again, looking directly at her. She started for a moment, then recovered. It had only been a coincidence. He couldn't see her.

She focused on him again. Yes, it was Fleming. The rogue Security Police officer who had been involved in the conspiracy she and James had uncovered around New Year's. The man who'd made her miserable at Edison. Who'd sold Martian hardware on the black market and was likely responsible for making it possible for Nikola Tesla to kill hundreds with the fire he'd started.

Fleming had been working with the aliens—or at least on their behalf—and now here he was, stealing people out of the city.

Susan shivered as questions raced through her mind. What did Fleming want with these people? Did this have something to do with what happened to Ben Johnson? Was Fleming working with the Martians, like some people had suspected? Were they preparing to attack the United States? And what did kidnapping random people from the streets have to do with an attack?

Should Susan report this to the SPs? No. Fleming might still be working for them. She needed to take this to Carl. He'd know what to do.

She watched as the prisoners were all loaded onto the boat while Fleming finished talking to one of the minders. He returned to his cart, and the minder jogged onto the watercraft and cast off the last line. Then Fleming's cart rode away, while the boat, with its cargo of prisoners, headed south on the East River.

CHAPTER 18

"Have you lost your mind, young lady?" Sam rumbled the next day.

Susan stuck out her chin in defiance. "Young lady? Don't 'young lady' me, old man. I received a tip and followed up on it, like any reporter would." She'd rehearsed this conversation in her mind on the way to the office and she wasn't going to let Sam rattle her, especially not in her morgue.

"But you're not a reporter, and you're not—"

"A man?" Susan interjected. "Go ahead, say it. Women don't belong out on the streets, especially at night. Right, Sam?"

"This isn't about women's suffrage, and you're not Inez Milholland, young—"

"Don't you dare 'young lady me' again, or I swear I'll throttle you where you stand," Susan growled.

"He might keel over from a stroke if you keep cutting him off," Carl said, grinning as he stepped out of the elevator. "Now, before I have to separate you two, can we discuss the more pressing matter at hand?"

Susan scowled. She didn't like Carl stepping in and acting like he was the only reasonable party when Sam was belittling and baiting her.

"Now, let me make sure I understand," Carl continued. "Sean Fleming. With SPs in uniform? Escorting prisoners onto a boat headed downstream on the East River?"

"I'm not entirely sure they were in uniform," Susan said, still upset but placated by getting back to the point. "They seemed to at least be wearing SP-issued gear, like boots."

"This poses more questions than it answers," Carl said, stroking his chin. "And we can't go to press with this. No corroboration, and if we did have it, the SPs could shut us down and lock us up. Is Fleming still working for the SPs? Or is he working with a group of castoffs? And why is he . . . abducting people? Or taking prisoners? Where is he taking them?"

"Do you have any contacts in the SPs who can tell you anything?" Susan asked.

"Oh sure!" Carl mimed holding a telephone up to his ear. "'Hey Bill, you seen Fleming lately? Any idea why he's grabbing people in New York and sending them down the river?'"

Susan crossed her arms and looked askance at Carl.

"That's a conversation that, at best, burns a contact," he said. "At worst, it gets me thrown in prison. And no, my contact's name isn't Bill."

"We need to know where they're taking the people," Sam said.

"That would be a start." Carl looked back at Susan. "How big was the boat?"

"About the size of the Hudson ferries?" Susan said, not sure how boats were measured.

"So they're taking the people to somewhere nearby," Carl said. "If they're taking them somewhere far away, they'd switch to a larger ship or a train."

"Then follow the boat," Sam said. "They're doing this late at night. A couple of men in small boats could track them at least out to the Narrows, if they go that far."

"You think they're going south?" Carl asked.

"They would have headed up the East River to Harlem if

they were going north. Upstream over there is easier than the Hudson. They'd save some fuel."

"I thought you were in the cavalry and not a sailor?"

"Doesn't mean I haven't been fishing."

"Well, first step is finding out how often they are doing this, so we need to get someone to watch the warehouse. From there, we can figure out when and how to follow the boat."

"That's it?" Susan asked. "Watch and wait?" People were being smuggled to God-knows-where, and Carl was talking about waiting for the next boat?

"What would you like to do?" Carl asked.

"Print a story?" Susan said. "Tell the families?"

"You want to print this story? With only you as a witness? If Fleming is working for the SPs, we're accusing them of kidnapping. If he's not, we're making them look like fools. Even if we had more than one witness, where do you think that gets us?"

Tears of frustration welled in Susan's eyes, but she choked them back. She wasn't going to cry in front of Sam, not after he'd called her "young lady."

"Likewise with telling the families," Sam said. "John Sumner gets wind of that, and we—along with the families—might find out where those people are being taken the hard way." John Sumner was the head of the Security Police and the real power behind the Bryan administration. He'd taken the helm after Anthony Comstock had retired and, to the shock of many, was even more heavy-handed than President Bryan's original "top cop."

"We were able to break the story with the radios because you, James, and Captain Reynolds found the rogue transmitter and pulled it off the air," Carl said. "That forced the government's hand, because once the rest of the stations on Planetary Warning heard what happened, the cat was out of the bag. We need to do something similar. So we need to learn more. I can start by visiting Pier 55 today and poking around, but we need coverage at night."

"The newsboys can help," Sam said. "I'll get someone posted at that old brewery. You said Broome and East Streets, Susan?"

"Newsboys?" Susan asked.

"Kids," Carl said. "Mostly boys and orphans. They sell papers and run errands for us."

"You're going to put children in danger?"

"They've been in danger since the day they were born," Sam said. "But they make great spies and informants because they're all but invisible."

Susan frowned. Another hard truth.

"I don't know what to wish for," Carl said. "We need to see enough kidnappings to figure out a pattern and arrange for someone to follow them. But that doesn't mean I want to see another twenty-four people taken tonight."

"Maybe we can speed up the process," Sam said. "I can talk to Fratelli and see if he'll put a boat out there for a few nights. He owes me one."

"You want to bring the mob into this?" Carl asked. "We just talked about how dangerous it is to spread this story."

"Who hates the SPs more than the mob?" Sam asked. "My biggest problem will be keeping Fratelli from storming the pier and killing Fleming."

"And what am I going to do while we wait for answers?" Susan asked.

Carl grinned. "I need you to ask a cruise line about your missing and presumed lost husband."

CHAPTER 19

Susan had loved playing dress up as a girl, and she still enjoyed putting on her Sunday best for a holiday or a night on the town. But now she was wearing a dress worth nearly six months of her salary, heels designed to make her calves ache, and a hat that would have sent Jill and Maggie into a storm of giggles.

And while putting on fancy clothes and playing pretend had been one of Susan's favorite games as a little girl, fantasizing about being the wife of a missing financier had never come to mind. She was blazing a new trail with this game—one that could lead her to jail, or the front page of one of *The Spectator*'s competitors. But if this was the price she had to pay to uncover another Martian conspiracy and keep Carl focused on the disappearances, she'd pay it.

She approached the Cunard Lines ticketing office, fighting the urge to spread her arms and maintain balance on remarkably impractical, stratospheric heels. But when she arrived, the door attendant bowed smartly, pulled the massive carved wooden door open, and gestured for her to enter. Susan's masquerade was working.

Cunard Lines sold tickets at their pier on the Hudson, but

they maintained a luxury Park Avenue office for their first-class passengers. The ticket office was what you'd expect of an exclusive location: a door attendant, who had already ushered Susan inside; a picturesque tiled floor that made her afraid she'd twist an ankle in her senseless shoes; and furniture intended for decoration, not sitting. Still, this was where Rose DiCaprio, wife of a prominent J.P. Morgan & Company executive, would go to demand answers about her missing husband.

"Good morning!" said a young woman dressed in the navy blue skirt, white blouse, and jacket of a female Cunard employee. "How can I help you, ma'am?"

"I am looking for information about my husband," Susan said. She'd debated trying to put on an upper-class accent, but she'd ultimately decided that Mrs. DiCaprio was from New Jersey and had met her Lawrence while working at the Knickerbocker Country Club across the river.

The young woman tilted her head, as if asking for more information.

"Lawrence DiCaprio," Susan added. "My Lawrence was on the *Mauretania*."

The young woman's eyes opened wide. She stepped forward, close enough that Susan could read the name Julia on her brass name tag. Julia placed a gentle hand on Susan's shoulder and said, "Let's head to my office, Mrs. DiCaprio. We can talk there."

Susan followed Julia to a windowless room with a small oak desk facing a pair of matching chairs. The desk was clear, the tile was spotless, and the creamy finish on the chairs was polished to a sheen. Were Cunard's cruise ships that luxurious? Susan had often daydreamed about taking a cruise to Europe with James for their honeymoon, but those days were part of a forgotten future now. They would have been lucky to travel in third class anyway.

"Can I get you something to drink, Mrs. DiCaprio?" Julia asked. "Coffee? Tea?"

"Tea, please," Susan said, sitting in one of the chairs facing the desk. "With milk and sugar." Rose DiCaprio didn't drink black tea.

Julia left the room. After a few moments, she reemerged with tea and service on a silver tray. She placed the tray on the desk and served the drink, complete with a pair of shortbread cookies, with practiced ease.

"Thank you," Susan said. She wasn't accustomed to being served like this, especially when she was impersonating a grieving, potential widow.

Julia sat down before speaking. "It must be so hard to not know where your husband is, Mrs. DiCaprio," she said. "Cunard is doing everything they can to determine what is happening with the *Mauretania*. We're working with the British navy to scour the English Channel for signs of our ship."

Her statement sounded practiced, even memorized. She'd probably spoken to ten other grieving family members this week. But she still sounded genuinely sad for "Rose."

For a moment, Susan felt that she shouldn't be there. She shouldn't be impersonating a woman who'd lost her husband on that ship. But she needed to get Carl what he wanted so that he'd help her.

And the English Channel? The cruise ship's route had been changed again? According to the information Susan had found before leaving for the Cunard office, its course was Liverpool, England; Queenstown, Ireland; and then across the ocean to New York. Carl had mentioned it had been rerouted to Halifax, Nova Scotia, but that was a minor adjustment, since all the ships crossed the Atlantic between Ireland and Newfoundland, just north of Nova Scotia. How would it end up in the English Channel?

"You said the Channel?" Susan asked as she sipped the tea. It was fantastic. "But the news says it was lost in the Atlantic. Was it rerouted? In distress when it went down?"

Julia winced. She looked straight ahead for a moment before

standing up and closing the office door. Then she sat in the chair next to Susan.

"I'm very sorry, Mrs. DiCaprio," Julia said. "I . . . I just learned this morning about the ship being rerouted to Cherbourg, and I misspoke. I'm not sure I'm supposed to be aware of the change in course, let alone share it. I hope I can count on your discretion?"

Well. This was a remarkable stroke of luck. Carl's ruse had been worth it.

"I don't know why it was sent to France," Julie went on. "But I have heard of ships being rerouted before, and it often means the government is involved, but please don't quote me on that." For a moment, the request made Susan think she had seen through her disguise, but Julia added, "The Royal Navy has one of their airships and a few airplanes to scout the area off France, since it disappeared so soon after the extra stop."

Airships? Did they think the *Mauretania* was still above water? This was where Susan would have cried if she could have, but she'd always found it hard to do so on demand. That was another skill that would have made Jill a better candidate for a reporter than Susan.

"Oh, that does make me feel better about the effort going into finding them," Susan said. "Thank you for confiding in me. I didn't realize they would use flying craft to search for a ship." She raised her voice into almost, but not quite, a question at the end.

"Well, no effort is being spared to find such an important vessel," Julia said. "And they might find . . . something more quickly with eyes in the air." Her effort to avoid the words *wreckage* and *debris* was almost visible.

"And how long does it normally take to find a missing ship like this?" Susan asked.

"Well, this has been an unusual situation," Julia said. "From what I have heard, they would have usually found . . . um, something by now."

Dealing with grieving families like this must have been difficult. Susan figured that "Rose DiCaprio" wasn't the first spouse or child who had sat in Julia's office, sipping tea.

"Do you think Cunard will tell the fam—I mean, us right away when they find something?" Susan fought the urge to wipe her brow. She'd slipped up. "What if it's related to the war in Europe? Or the return of the Martians?"

Julia leaned back in her chair. One of her eyebrows tilted up for a second, then corrected itself. "I don't think Cunard would try to conceal anything from families who are worried about their missing loved ones, Mrs. *DiCaprio,*" Julia said with just the slightest emphasis on the last name of Susan's alter ego. "But if someone decides it's a national security issue, it would be out of our hands."

Susan nodded and took a nervous sip of tea. She'd tipped her hand, but Julia had made a mistake, too. Had they reached a stalemate?

"Did I hear from someone in your household yesterday?" Julia asked.

Was this a test? Carl had anticipated this. Time to see if his strategy would work, or if he would be bailing Susan out of the Tombs.

"My household?" Susan said. "I don't think so." Short and sweet. Bad liars always said too much, according to Carl.

"Okay. I'm sorry I can't tell you more, Mrs. DiCaprio. Do you need a few more minutes?"

The tea was excellent, but "short and sweet" counted toward this meeting, too. "No, thank you," Susan said, rising from her chair. "I feel much better now, Julia. You've been very helpful."

Julia led her out of the office and back into the lobby, where they said their farewells. Then Susan left, walked half a block, and breathed a deep sigh of relief. *Spectator* headquarters was nearby, and she couldn't wait to get out of those heels.

"Excuse me. Mrs. DiCaprio?"

Susan turned and faced a tall, middle-aged man. He was wearing a fine silk suit and a matching hat, and sported a perfectly trimmed mustache. If he didn't work for Cunard, then he was one of its first-class passengers. Was he an acquaintance of Lawrence DiCaprio's? Was Susan about to be caught?

"Yes?" she said, already afraid of the man's response.

"You're looking for information about your missing husband?" he said.

"Yes, I am. But I don't see how that's any of your—"

"I can help you," he said as he placed one hand on Susan's shoulder.

"Don't touch me!" she exclaimed, violently shrugging the man off and facing him. He had at least a couple of inches of height on her, but she could make up for it in menace.

"I'm sorry," the man said, holding up his hands to show that they were empty. "I shouldn't have grabbed you like that. Please excuse me. I can tell you what happened to him . . . and why."

Susan crossed her arms. The man looked back at her and wrinkled his brow, as if waiting for her to speak.

"Well?" Susan finally said. She was convinced this man was some kind of hustler, but he'd called her by her assumed name, so he must have overheard something inside the Cunard office.

"I can't tell you here. Someone might—"

"You can't tell me here," Susan said. "Imagine that! Shame on you, sir. I don't know what you want, and I'm sure I don't want to know. Taking advantage of a grieving widow like this? I should call a police officer." She raised her voice on the word *police* while putting her hand up to project the sound. A pair of passersby slowed down to glance at her.

"No, please," the man said, producing a business card. "Come to this address. Tomorrow night at eight o'clock. It's a public place, and you can bring a guest, if that makes you feel more safe."

Susan took the card. It gave an address on East 34th Street, but nothing else. By the time she was done reading it and looked up, the man was receding into a crowd on the other side of Park Avenue. Her heart was still pounding when she reached *Spectator* headquarters.

CHAPTER 20

Susan sat next to Sam inside Jasper's office, watching Carl play with the tuning control on the radio unit. Word was that the national network was broadcasting periodic messages as part of an initial test.

"You're not going to pick up Sayville," Susan snapped. "That's not how radios work. The only station you'll find is the one on the card in the package." She didn't want to teach Carl to use a radio. She needed to talk to him about the *Mauretania* and gather any new information about Sean Fleming's kidnappings.

"So why is it adjustable?" Jasper asked.

"Probably to make it easier to shift to a new frequency because of transmitter issues, weather interference, or some other reason," Susan said. "I think they're using different settings west of here."

"You understand all this voodoo?" Sam asked.

Susan laughed. "Some of it, yes. It's not complicated once you understand the basics."

"—sident Bryan has been nominated for the Nobel Peace Prize for his efforts in bringing peace to Mexico after the German invasion in 1910," the radio said after Carl put it back on the correct frequency.

"Oh bull—I mean, poppycock," Sam said, looking nervously at Susan as he talked over the radio.

"You can say 'bullshit,' Sam," she said. "My ears won't melt."

Sam's mouth hung open in surprise as Carl laughed.

"—in Europe, the Martians have been all but destroyed by the courageous French, Italian, and Austrian armies," the radio continued. "Their working together, with the help of our valiant advisers, to rout the last few clusters of alien—"

Carl, no longer laughing, switched the radio off.

"What are you doing?" Jasper exclaimed. "It was working."

"It's what I predicted," Carl said. "And what Susan said: Bullshit."

Susan wasn't sure she deserved the credit, but Carl's stone-faced expression showed that he wasn't up for banter.

"We all know Bryan had nothing to do with peace in Mexico," Carl said. "That war never ended, and the Germans still occupy Chiapas and the Yucatán. But I can tell you right now that the French, Italian, and Austrian armies are not working together. There are no French or Austrian armies. Both of those countries were nearly leveled by the Martians, and no one can tell you what's happening in Italy."

"The person I spoke to at Cunard told me the *Mauretania* was rerouted to Cherbourg, France," Susan said. "That's where they're looking for the ship. Was it sent there to pick up survivors?"

"I knew it," Carl said. "I still don't know what they were picking up, but whatever it was, it got them killed."

Sam whistled.

"There must be some sort of provisional government operating from the coast," Carl continued. "And while their capital is being run by gangs, they're relaxing on the beach. But that might explain why the ship was sent into the Channel."

"So those briefings about it sinking in the Atlantic were all lies?" Jasper asked.

"Seems so," Susan said. "But the woman at Cunard wasn't supposed to tell me that. She only overheard it herself."

"Really?" Jasper said. "So Cunard's management are being told one thing, while the public hears another."

"Some of Cunard's people need to be in the know and are bad at keeping secrets," Carl said. "But a few leaks here and there don't hurt the government much. And now they have this." He pointed at the radio. "They can control the narrative even more tightly. Just repeat their lies often enough, and they become the truth."

"So what do you think we should do with this monstrosity, then?" Sam asked, gesturing toward the radio. "Pitch it out the window?"

"No," Jasper answered. "We set it up in a quiet room and have stenographers log what they say. But none of it will be printed without editorial review." Jasper held up a hand to silence Carl, who'd opened his mouth in protest. "We're not going to turn into a mouthpiece for the government. I'll leave that to the *Post* and the *Times*."

"We need to figure out how to tell people that what they're hearing is lies," Carl exclaimed. "They're talking about distributing one of these to every household in the country by the end of the year!"

"That's impossible," Susan said. "That's, what . . . twenty million units? The most that General Electric could promise was forty thousand a month, and even that was a stretch."

"So?" Carl said, hands held out in frustration. "They're lying. We've covered that. Either way, we can't stand by and let them spread this garbage. It's bad enough with the national papers already acting as their stenographers. Now we will, too?"

"I'm talking about recording the lies for now, Carl," Jasper said. "We'll figure out in good time how to use them without fighting over the top bunk with my dad's buddy Randolph." He walked to his office door. "Joan? Find a place for this radio and . . ." His voice trailed off as he left the room.

"Any word on Pier 55, Sam?" Susan asked, taking advantage of the natural break.

"Fratelli's boys followed a boat with about thirty prisoners on it last night," Sam said. "It headed south, like we expected, and then took the Arthur Kill inland. They had to break off as soon as they hit Newark Bay, though."

Susan frowned.

"It's not all bad," Carl said. "The mob is interested in helping. They're working with their associates in Staten Island and New Jersey on posting lookouts to follow the next 'shipment.'"

"Yeah, they're all willing to put aside their differences to take on a common enemy," Sam added. "No one kidnaps people around here without paying their dues."

"Seriously?" Susan asked, her lip curling. "That's what they're worried about?"

"Strange bedfellows, if you'll pardon the pun," Sam said.

"That's not a pun, but you're pardoned," Carl said. "Yes, we should learn more in the next few days."

"I do have one more bit of information from Cunard, but I think it's nothing," Susan said, holding out the business card that the man outside the cruise line office had given her.

"What's this?" Carl said, snatching the card from Susan's hand.

Susan described her encounter outside the Cunard office.

"Ah, he was just some crackpot," Sam scoffed.

"I think he's preying on the families of people lost on the cruise," Susan said.

"What do you mean?" Carl asked.

"It's not obvious? He used my—Rose's—name. He promised me information about my missing husband. He's a hustler. A confidence man."

"City's full of 'em," Sam said.

Carl nodded.

"This isn't news?" Susan asked. "The largest cruise ship in

the world isn't declared lost yet, and there's already someone trying to steal—or worse—from the widows?"

"It's news," Carl said. "I can ask the city editor to put someone on it."

"But he'll be looking for me," Susan said.

"And that's why you won't be going, missy," Sam said.

Susan spun and looked daggers at him.

"No, she's right," Carl said behind her. "Rose DiCaprio should go if she wants. And if you're really worried, her father can go, too."

CHAPTER 21

The address on East 34th Street was a storefront with an ineptly whitewashed sign that used to read Joe's Haberdashery. Susan, wearing the tasteful black that Rose DiCaprio might pick for this somber occasion, stepped inside with Sam—or rather, "Rose's father"—right behind.

The inside of the store was larger than Susan had expected. The former sales floor still had the cabinets, shelves, and hangers for displaying men's wear, but neatly aligned rows of folding chairs covered most of the open space. Many of the seats were filled. Carl had been right; it wasn't meant to be a private meeting. Good. Susan could grab a seat, figure out what it was about, and escape without facing that grabby creep again.

She made a quick count before she selected a chair three rows from the back. Forty-three people, most of them well-dressed. Many were whispering to each other as if this wasn't their first meeting.

"It's like a church," Sam said as he took a seat next to her.

He was right. It felt like Redeemer Baptist's sinister older brother. Only with a better-dressed and—upon closer inspection by Susan—exclusively white congregation. Had the man invited

"Rose" here for her spiritual benefit? Had he been trying to help her?

"But there's no cross," Sam added. "No signs. No hymnals."

"There might be no service today," Susan said. "This might be a meeting for people related to passengers on the ship. We can get an idea of what they're discussing and slip out when we have enough for Carl."

Sam nodded.

After a few moments, the man who'd approached Susan stepped to the front of the room, stood behind a small lectern, and held up his hands for the audience's attention.

"Good evening, everyone," he said. "Hail Ares! Thank you for being here."

"Hey Larry's?" Sam asked.

No. Susan had unmistakably heard "Hail Ares." What could that possibly mean?

"I see a healthy number of new faces here!" the speaker continued. "For those of you who don't know me, my name is Nathan Filby, the vicar of New York's First Church of Ares. I'm excited for you all to hear from our leader, Father Percival Howell. And without further ado, here he is!"

Nathan stepped aside and took a seat to make way for Father Percival, an older gentleman wearing a black suit cut more for the turn of the century than for 1915. His bald pate was ringed with hair stained with boot black that matched a wispy goatee. His jacket was buttoned all the way up, drawing the eye to a dark red cravat matching the red cuff links that poked out of his sleeves when he gestured with his arms. And gesture he did. He waved his arms like a Coney Island carnival barker, selling tickets for the eight-armed man from Mars.

"Ladies and gentlemen, seekers of truth, children of the Red Earth, welcome!" Father Percival said, pausing as if for dramatic effect. "We gather today beneath the banner of Ares, the flame-forged god who watches over war, and peace, and renewal. Today, the world still trembles from the echo of the Second Great

Martian Storm that is scarring our skies in Europe. The iron clatter of their machines, the thunderous roar of their heat rays, and the haunting silence that followed were myths we whispered around hearths and the nightmares that haunted our dreams."

He paused to survey his congregation. As he did, a subdued hum emanated from behind him. It was barely noticeable, but Susan, who was used to spending time in the labs at Edison, was reminded of the noise James and Seward were trying to eliminate from their devices.

"Yet within those myths lies a promise," Father Percival went on. "A prophecy carved in the ancient tablets of our forebears and etched in the canals of our father's planet: the true children of Ares shall return, not as conquerors, but as harbingers of a new age. And they are here! The faithful did not fear the unknown; they embraced it, and they will be rewarded! We do not await salvation from distant stars, nor do we cower before celestial fire. Instead, we prepare our souls, our communities, and our very spirits to greet them with open arms and reverent hearts."

By this point, Father Percival had raised his voice, and Susan noticed that the humming had increased ever so slightly with it. Where was the humming coming from? James and Seward had experimented with a few different recording technologies. Ben Johnson had also adapted some of the Martian technology to record sound signals onto shellac cylinders before Susan and James were even out of school and working at Edison. At one point, James had been tasked with reviving the project for playback on the radio. Was someone recording this meeting with ill-behaved equipment?

"The return of the Martians marks the crucible in which humanity's destiny will be forged," Father Percival droned on. "Like the forge of Hephaestus, the trials they bring will melt away our petty divisions, temper our resolve, and reveal the true mettle of humankind: courage, compassion, and unity under a common sky."

Susan recalled how many new religions had sprung up after the first Martian Attack, but most had died off since then. President Bryan and Anthony Comstock, both ardent Christians, had helped many of those religions to their graves. Sometimes literally. It made Susan a little nervous to merely be in this room.

The droning sound persisted, growing a little bit louder but somehow increasing in intensity, making Susan's head ache.

"Brothers and sisters, the drums of destiny beat louder each day," Father Percival went on. "You have heard the lies about the defeat of our saviors in Europe. Ignore them! They cannot be beaten! They must be welcomed when they arrive here!" He paused again for dramatic effect, but the droning continued.

"Let's go," Susan whispered to Sam. "That sound is hurting my head. Do you hear it?"

Sam was staring straight ahead, as if completely enthralled by Father Percival.

"Hey, you're not really listening to this guy, are you?" Susan asked. "Let's go."

Sam didn't respond. He didn't acknowledge Susan at all. He only stared straight ahead, as if in a trance. The entire room was still, with everyone in the congregation facing forward in the same apparent daze. Was it the droning? Did the sound have some kind of hypnotic effect on the audience? Why not on Susan, though?

Father Percival continued on with his own, presumably less dangerous droning, while Nathan Filby watched from his seat. Susan noticed that Nathan didn't appear to be enthralled. Instead, he was scanning the room.

Susan sat up straight and leveled her head. What now? Wait and see? Was this part of the kidnappings? Were they using this terrible technology to snare the victims before putting them in chains? No. This was the wrong neighborhood, and the wrong people. But that didn't mean she and Sam weren't in serious danger.

Father Percival had now moved on from how glorious the invaders were to how they would punish the unfaithful. Nathan Filby scanned the crowd one more time, then rose and stepped out of the room through the curtain Father Percival had come in through. If Susan was going to get herself and Sam out of here, it would have been now.

"Sam!" she hissed, elbowing the big man in the ribs. Nothing. Would she need to stab or shoot him to wake him—

Stab! She still had extra hairpins with her for that ridiculous hat she'd had to wear to Cunard.

She fished a pin out of her purse, struggling to stay as still as possible in case Father Percival was watching. Then, praying that she wouldn't create more danger than they were already in, she poked Sam in the thigh.

Sam jumped, looked at Susan, and opened his mouth.

"Shhhh," she hissed.

"But—"

"Shush. You were asleep. We need to leave as quickly and quietly as possible."

"Bu—" Sam's eyes had already begun to glaze over.

Susan punched the spot on his thigh where she'd stabbed him with the hairpin. "Now," she whispered firmly enough that he rose.

They crept to the exit. Susan risked a single glance back, but Father Percival continued preaching.

Once they slipped out the door, Susan herded a still-stunned Sam to 3rd Avenue. She looked back down East 34th and saw a man exit the old storefront. She started to tell Sam to run, then watched the other man hastily flee in the opposite direction. Maybe Susan hadn't been the only person immune to whatever that terrifying sound was.

"Want to tell me what the hell is going on?" Sam asked as

Susan turned back toward him. "And why the hell did you stab me, missy?"

CHAPTER 22

Susan shuffled the papers on her desk for the fifth time in as many minutes. She knew it had been five minutes, because she'd been checking the clock on the morgue wall every thirty seconds. She'd survived a bombing. She'd helped escort marines to a gunfight with rogue SP agents. She'd been in her elementary school when the Martians had attacked her hometown just a few blocks away. But nothing had shaken her like the hypnotic device she and Sam had escaped last night.

As she and Sam had hustled across town to her apartment, Susan had explained what had happened. Sam had resisted coming upstairs to her place ("That wouldn't be proper!"), but she'd refused to go up alone, even though common sense told her that Nathan Filby—if that was his real name—knew her as Rose DiCaprio, not Susan Wilson.

But even if Susan wasn't in any personal danger, the whole country—if not the whole continent—was. Who created that device? Was it Martian technology? Or a human creation based on it? What would happen if someone connected that device to the National Radio Network? What were the consequences of extended exposure? Would people become more suggestible? Or simply catatonic? Susan had briefly considered throwing the radio unit in the stenography room out the window on her way up to the morgue that morning.

And why hadn't the device worked on her and the other man who had escaped? The only person who might be able to tell her something was James. She hated the idea of seeing him at all, much less asking him for help. But this wasn't about her. It was about a deadly weapon that could threaten the entire country.

She picked up her desk telephone.

"Operator," said the cheerful voice on the other end.

Susan gave her the number for her desk at Edison. They must have someone answering it by now.

"Edison Laboratories, Radio Division," said a strange voice. It sounded like a woman who'd been smoking cigarettes since the War of the Rebellion.

"Yes, I'd like to speak to J—Mr. Brogan, please," Susan said, putting on her most professional tone.

"May I ask who's calling, please?"

"This is Karen Wagner at General Electric. I need to discuss the transformer requirements for the latest design." As far as Susan knew, there was no Karen Wagner at GE.

"Well, for logistics questions, you should speak to Mr. Abrams," her replacement rasped. "He's right here."

"No, this is for Mr. Brogan's ears only," Susan insisted, using a tone that had usually helped her break past gatekeepers when she'd called on James's or Ben Johnson's behalf before.

"Well, he's not here. I can take a message."

"Will he be in today?"

"No, he's out."

Susan started to ask where he was, but realized it might cause a stir if James returned to an urgent message from GE. "Okay then," she said. "I will, uh, try Mr. Abrams later. Thank you."

She'd have to head back to New Jersey to track James down on his way to work—or even at home, where Susan would have to face his mother. That was not something Susan was looking forward to. But this was important, and she could try to see Jill and Maggie.

The elevator door slid open a few unproductive minutes after Susan had hung up, and Carl strode off. "So?" he asked.

"So?" Susan asked right back.

"Last night? What happened?" Carl held up his hands with his palms facing out.

"You haven't spoken to Sam?"

"He's not in yet."

Susan's heart leaped into her throat. It was already 9:35 a.m. Sam usually beat Susan into the office. Had something happened to him? Did the horrible device have some kind of aftereffect?

"Are you okay, Susan?" Carl asked. "Sam's on Staten Island. Or on his way back by now, I hope. He's meeting with one of his contacts. I think something happened with the boats last night."

Susan breathed a sigh of relief and recounted what had happened the night before.

"The First Church of Ares?" Carl asked.

"You've heard of it?" Susan asked hopefully.

"No. But Percival's a distinct name. A confidence man using that name, and sporting a black goatee, worked Red Hook a few years ago. Sold a couple of factories."

"What's wrong with that?"

"Ask the guy who owned them," Carl quipped. "I think you and Sam walked into a scam. You said that guy Filby was a creep? You were right."

"You think this was a scam?" Susan asked. "You didn't see what I saw, Carl. Those people were entranced. I don't know what they're planning, but this is terrifying."

"I've seen what skilled speakers can do to a crowd, Susan. They take advantage of rhythm. They choose their words. It's not hard; they've upgraded to some kind of scientific music or something."

"It's more than that, Carl, I mean it. Talk to Sam when he gets here. We can't let them connect this to the radio network. And I need to talk to James. Maybe he knows of some Martian tech they uncovered in the wreckage that points to this. Or it might be something new."

"James? Absolutely not. He talks to Ross. Ross talks to Washington. The SPs will be on us like flies on manure, and we'll have to burn half of the stories we're working on."

"No, I can trust James." But Susan realized how ridiculous that sounded as the words left her mouth. Of course she couldn't.

The elevator door slid open again, and Sam walked into the morgue.

"How do you feel?" Susan asked.

"A little bit of a headache," Sam said. "Whatever the hell that was did a number on me, but we got bigger fish to fry."

"Bigger fish? Than that?"

"Yeah. Got that map?"

Susan set aside some papers and produced a map of the waterways near New York City.

"The Staten Island mob picked up last night's boat of captives here," Sam said, pointing to Shooter's Island, a small piece of land sitting north of Staten Island between Kill Van Kull and Newark Bay. "They followed it north into Newark Bay. According to the survivor, they made it pretty far, past the Singer factory here." He pointed to an area labeled Elizabeth on the west side of the bay.

"Survivor?" Carl asked.

"I'm gettin' to it," Sam said. "They had Newark on their port, he said, and Kearny Point was just about in view when the boat opened fire on them." He glanced up from the map and looked them both in the eye—first Susan, then Carl.

"My God, only one survived?" Susan said. First the hypnotic sound device, now a ship full of men killed. They had been criminals, but that didn't mean they deserved to drown or be shot.

"Yep," Sam said. "And he's got one hell of a story. I reckon we may have an idea of why they opened fire, too."

"There's more?" Carl asked.

"Poor kid was a swab. Survived the sinking of the *Connecticut* off the coast of Mexico so he could get sunk again in goddamn Newark Bay! Anyway, he swam ashore around here, near the mouth of the Passaic River, where there shouldn't be anything. Except there was."

"Huh?" Carl said.

"Once you're past the shipyards"—Sam pointed at the spot on the map—"there's a whole lot of nothing. It's too far from the railroads. Swampy. Fields. The kid came ashore around here, I guess, and walked inland toward Newark to hitch a ride back home."

"Makes sense," Carl said.

"But he saw lights," Sam said. "Lots of 'em. Over on Kearny Point. The Martians made it that far when they attacked the first time and wiped the area out. No one's ever rebuilt there because the railroad gave Newark and Elizabeth better access. But someone's doing something out there now. I bet it's got something to do with our missing people."

Something rang familiar to Susan as she examined the map. She followed Sam's finger to a peninsula sitting between the Passaic River and the Newark Bay.

Kearny Point. Carny.

"Kearny!" she read out loud.

Carl and Sam both gave her puzzled expressions.

"General Ross's new driver mentioned Kearny," Susan explained. "Then he clammed up because he wasn't supposed to talk about it." Was there a secret military base right here in the States? Right next to the city? And were the SPs kidnapping people and imprisoning them there?

"That's a hell of a coincidence," Carl said, narrowing his eyes as if in concentration.

"Did you two talk about last night?" Sam said. "I don't know what the hell they did to me, but it wasn't good."

"You too, Sam?" Carl said without looking up from his ruminations. "You guys were reeled in by some soothsayer."

"I worked that séance story with you a couple of years ago, remember?" Sam said. "The woman with those drugged candles? I played the father with the lost daughter. This is different."

"How so?"

"That time I saw stuff, and her routine kinda put me into a state. Like just enough shots of rye, but not too many. Last night, I was out of it. Gone." Sam pulled over a chair and sat down. "I'm still a little tired, to be honest."

"So we've got a new military installation in Jersey and some kind of hypnotizing device in the city," Carl said as he put his hands in his pockets and leaned against the morgue's counter. "Busy week."

"How can you be so nonchalant?" Susan said. "The SPs are kidnapping people and bringing them there! And you're not taking what we saw last night seriously."

"We don't have evidence that those people are being taken by the SPs, and we're not sure they're being taken to Kearny Point," Carl said. "And I don't know what to think about last night, Susan."

"We need to go back to Thirty-Fourth Street and poke around," Sam said. "That thing is, at a minimum, dangerous. The cops wouldn't believe us if we filed some kinda report—at least not until we dig enough up for a decent story."

"Not a bad idea," Carl said. "Are you game to go back there late tonight, Sam?"

"Yeah. I'd like to know a little more about the people who tried to hypnotize me."

"Can we get close enough to Kearny Point to take a look beforehand?" Susan asked.

"I don't know about that," Sam replied. "If they were willing to open fire on—Wait. *We?*"

"Yes, we," Susan said. There it was, the inevitable "this is too dangerous for women" speech.

"You're not—" Sam started to say

"If you're going anywhere to investigate electronic equipment, you need me," Susan cut him off. "I know more about radios than anyone in this building. I'm also immune to whatever it did to you, Sam. You only got out of there because I woke you up. So I am going back to that Church of Ares, too." She crossed her arms.

Sam stared back at her blankly.

"Well, that settles that," Carl said. "We'll head over around nine tonight."

"But what about the kidnappings?" Susan asked.

"Sam is right," Carl answered. "Whoever was piloting that boat opened fire on another craft just for getting too close. I need to talk to my Coast Guard contacts, and I might risk a couple of calls to some military informants."

Susan frowned.

"You want to do something right away," Carl said.

She nodded.

"Welcome to my life," Carl said with a wistful grin.

CHAPTER 23

The streets were empty as Susan, Carl, and Sam walked from the bus stop at 33rd Street and 3rd Avenue to the alley where they could gain access to the loading doors for the First Church of Ares. Curfew was less than an hour away, and the city was doing what it did best: adjusting.

The church's loading doors were outfitted with sturdy steel hasps sealed by new—and quite expensive-looking—locks. The entrance door on one side of the loading doors was similarly secure. But a vent window, barely wide enough for a small person, was tipped open.

"You know the drill, Carl," Sam said.

Carl sighed, then took off his hat and stained jacket.

"You've done this before?" Susan asked.

"Are you surprised?" Carl asked.

"No," Susan said, and shrugged. "But how will you climbing through the window do us any good?"

"There'll be a drawer, and that drawer will have keys," Sam said. "There always is."

Carl disappeared into the window, and three minutes later, Sam caught a set of keys on a ring. One opened the padlock, and Carl pushed open the door before Sam could unlock it. Sam pulled his pistol out of his jacket. Carl was already wielding one as he waited for them inside.

The back room still bore memories of its previous life, with a set of moth-eaten wool coats hanging against one wall, an array of silk ties, and a collection of red fedoras sitting in one corner.

"Red?" Sam asked. "Who the hell would wear a red fedora?"

Carl snorted.

A curtain at one end of the storage area led to the showroom-turned-nave where Susan and Sam had sat the night before. Susan led the way through. The lectern where Father Percival had preached from stood alone at that end of the room, but her eyes were drawn to a sheet draped over something short and wide, like a credenza or nightstand.

Pulling the sheet aside, Susan revealed a squat bookshelf stuffed with electronics equipment, including an uncovered speaker with a wide cone and an enormous magnet. She gestured for Carl and Sam to come over.

"Well, it was more than a typical scam," Carl said.

"You doubted us?" Sam asked.

"It's my job, Sam. You know that. Susan, you recognize anything?"

Susan's eyes were drawn to a box on the bottom shelf of the bookcase. She knelt down to inspect it more closely, hoping she was wrong. She wasn't.

A bead of sweat ran down her face. "This is an Edison amplifier," she said.

"Are you sure?" Carl asked.

"Positive. James designed this last year. We—uh, they manufacture these amplifiers for the military. It says 'Edison' right here." Susan pointed at the letters stamped on the amplifier's left side.

"How the hell did one end up over here?" Sam asked.

"Damn good question," Carl asked. "But we need to get the hell out of here. What else looks interesting, Susan?"

Susan traced a cable back from the amplifier to a small black metal box that had no controls or branding. It only had a connection to the amplifier and another to a GE power supply. "The power supply is from GE," she said. "Pretty standard model."

"Military?" Sam asked.

"Could be," Susan said. "Could be for industrial machines, signs. It's not hard to modify a power supply for something like—"

"Who's in there?" bellowed a familiar voice from the storeroom.

"Cops?" Sam whispered.

"No, that's Filby," Susan said.

Sam and Carl leveled their guns at the curtain as it swept aside. Nathan Filby moved toward them, brandishing a pistol of his own.

"Who the hell—oh, Mrs. DiCaprio," Filby said, placing sarcastic emphasis on Susan's alias. "I see you decided to come back. I don't know what kind of scam you're trying to run, but you have made a grave mistake."

"We've got you outgunned, Mr. Filby," Sam said. "No one has to get hurt here. Just put your weapon down, take a few steps back, and I'll even leave it by the door for you on our way out."

Filby laughed. "You see, that's part of your mistake. I'm not going to be alone for long. My boss will be here soon with a few men, and then you're going to take a little trip."

"Oh, is Father Percival going to come talk us to death?" Susan asked, winking at Carl as she grabbed the cable between the black box and the power supply.

"Father Percival?" Filby laughed again. "He's not the boss. He might think so, but he doesn't know what's going on, either. I work for someone much more terrifying than that."

"I knew a Percival once," Carl said. "Ran a bridge scam on Coney Island."

"Not bridge," Filby corrected him. "Commercial real estate. Small potatoes, perfect for him. No, I graduated to the big time now, buddy. You'll see. . . ." He went on a roll then, bragging about his prowess and how he'd finally had it made. He was so wrapped up in himself that he didn't notice how his gun had lowered a bit, which made it easier for Susan to stand and strike him in the face with the black box.

Filby's pistol clattered to the floor. Susan picked it up as he writhed in pain, both hands up to his face.

"Let's get the hell out of here," Carl said.

Sam scooped up the box as the three of them burst through the curtain, ran through the stockroom, and exited into the alley. Carl slowed as they reached 34th Street.

"I don't hear anything," he said. "Slow down. We'll attract less attention."

They fell into step, heading west at a brisk pace. But within a few seconds, lights from an approaching vehicle flashed, and Sam pushed them into a doorway.

"The curfew!" he said.

The vehicle was a sedan, but not a police car. It pulled up just short of the First Church of Ares, and two men got out. Susan immediately recognized the passenger.

"You have got to be kidding me," she said. "That's Sean Fleming."

CHAPTER 24

"They're distributing radios to households in New York, Newark, and Jersey City," Carl said as he stepped off the elevator and into the morgue.

"Hmm," said Susan, trying and failing to focus on the latest crossword.

"I said, they're distributing radios," Carl said, raising his voice a bit. He put his coffee cup on Susan's counter and tried to catch her eye.

"And I heard you," Susan said, mulling over six-letter words for *hopeless*.

"Nothing else to say?"

"What exactly do you want to hear? It's all . . . futile," she said, filling in the puzzle.

"Futile?"

"Sean Fleming is, as unbelievable as it sounds, still working for the Martians. We learned from those German soldiers who got through on Planetary Warning that someone over in Europe was, so why not here? He might be doing it on his own, but he's probably still working for the government. We know this because his secret base in New Jersey is a regular travel destination for General Ross. I can't tell if it makes a difference. Either way, whoever he's working for is going to broadcast some kind of mind control signal over the National Radio Network so the aliens can come eat us or something."

Susan looked up from the crossword puzzle at Carl. "Did I miss anything? Is there some gem of hope in there?"

"Nope, that about covers it," Carl said. "Although we don't know why he's been taking those people."

"To feed his alien masters?" Susan asked, choking back tears at the thought. Lisa Watts was dead. She'd failed to save her, if saving her had ever been possible. She'd need to go tell Anthony and Audrey so that at least they'd know the truth before the end.

Carl looked back at Susan, as if he were unsure of what to say.

"Hey, I opened this thing up," Sam said as he stepped off the elevator, the black box he'd taken from the Church of Ares in one hand. "What do you think?"

"Why?" Susan asked.

"Huh?" Sam said, stopping mid-stride.

"Why bother? What are we going to do with it?"

"Well, figure out what it does and how to stop it."

"It generates some frequency that interferes with how our brains work or something. The Martians must have figured it out. We know their technology is more advanced than ours."

"Well, look at it," Sam insisted. "You understand this stuff. There's got to be some way to stop it. It may be time to talk to that worthless ex-boyfriend of yours."

"We wouldn't need to stop that," Susan said. "We would need to stop the broadcast."

"You mean like they did," Carl said.

"What?" Susan asked, tilting her head.

"Stop the transmission," Carl clarified. "Or block it. Like they did to the radios at Sayville."

He was right. They *could* stop this. But they needed a transmitter. A powerful one. Like the one at Sayville.

"Could we use the one at Sayville?" Carl asked, as if reading Susan's mind.

"It could work," Susan said. "But how long would it take for the government to figure it out and take back control?"

"Then we need your boyfriend to make a new one," Sam said.

"That would require him being willing to go against the general, and I don't believe he's got the, um, courage for that," Susan said, letting the word *boyfriend* slide. "And I don't know how much time we have. This is just . . . futile." She rested her chin in one hand.

"It's not like you to give up," Carl said.

"It's my second alien conspiracy in less than a year. They're wearing me out." Susan cast her eyes down toward the black box Sam had placed on the counter and noticed a collection of electronics like she'd never seen before. "This is the box from last night?" she asked, even though she knew the answer.

"Yes," Sam said. "It was a bitch to get open, pardon the expression. They riveted the damn thing closed. I had to borrow a drill from the super."

Susan could pick out the capacitors, coils, diodes, and valves in the gear that James and Seward had built or tested at Edison. But the tiny disc and the wafer-shaped doodads in this little box were almost unrecognizable. James had found something odd when he'd sifted through the wreckage from the explosion at Coney Island, but he'd given it up to Fleming before he could finish inspecting it. Otherwise, James would have locked himself in one of his labs and starved himself while testing these circuits.

"You're thinking about something," Carl said.

Susan ignored Carl and kept her focus on the alien device. What would James do if he saw this? No good would come from seeing him again. Except, perhaps, a chance to stop—or at least hamper—whatever the aliens and their human assistants were planning. But Carl was right; James couldn't be trusted. He'd already proven that he was willing to manipulate her on General

Ross's orders. How could she be sure he wouldn't run right back to his boss?

Susan couldn't be sure. But so what if James did? Would things get much worse?

"I have an idea," she said. "But you're not going to like it."

CHAPTER 25

"I can't believe I let you talk me into this," Captain Reynolds said.

"*That* convinced you, not me," Susan said, pointing to the device Sam had swiped from the First Church of Ares.

"It did help," the marine captain said as he turned it around in his hands.

The door to the Sayville radio station office cracked open. "I see Hornburger's car down the road, sir," said one of the marine guards.

"Thank you," Reynolds said.

Susan took a deep breath as the guard closed the door behind himself. Aside from herself and Reynolds, the office was already empty. They'd decided that confronting James alone would be best. Convincing Sam and Carl that her plan was the only way to get James involved was hard enough. Convincing Reynolds had taken two days.

Susan held her hands behind her to conceal their shaking as a few minutes of uneasy silence passed. Finally, the sound of car wheels crunching on gravel bled through the closed door.

Would this work? Would James be convinced by the Martian electronics? Would Susan believe him if he said he was?

The door opened, and James entered the office. His hair was a mess, and a week's worth of beard made his cheeks appear unwashed. His shirt might have been pressed back in June or July. Wasn't his mother taking care of him? Susan had to suppress a smile at the thought. Getting James away from his mother, as much as Susan loved her, had always been the problem. Losing his father early had made him a bit too attached to her. Not quite a mama's boy, but almost.

"Captain Reynolds," James said. "Is everything okay in here? Why are your men—Susan?"

"James," Susan said, crossing her arms.

"What are you doing here?" he asked.

"Nice to see you, too."

"That's not what I meant," James sputtered. "I haven't seen you. I wanted to talk, but you . . . you just left. . . ."

"We're not here for that," Susan said, then pointed to the black chassis. "Look at that box."

"So the radios aren't down again?" James asked Reynolds.

"Look at the box," Reynolds said.

James sighed and stepped over to the chassis on the table. After a moment, he gasped. "Where did you find this?" he asked.

"Church," Susan said.

James looked up with a puzzled expression.

"It's a long story," Susan went on. "But before I go into it, I need you to promise to listen to the whole thing, because you're not going to like it."

James examined the box again, then gazed back at Susan and nodded.

"So Colonel Fleming is back, and General Ross is working with him?" James asked after Susan finished a condensed version of what had happened over the past few weeks.

"That's what it looks like," Susan said.

"And they're going to use the radios to control people," James said, his brow furrowed.

"It's incredible," Reynolds added, "but after what we saw last winter . . ."

"I don't blame you for being upset with the general, Susan, but . . ." James started.

"This has nothing to do with that," Susan said. "General Ross told you to do something underhanded and manipulative, but I'm more angry with you for going along with it than I am with him for suggesting it. Check that chassis again, James. That's all the evidence you need."

"You're talking about electronic mind control," James said. "That's not real life. That's fantasy, the stuff you'd find in a scientific romance."

Susan had half expected this from James, which was one of the reasons why she'd had Reynolds feign radio problems and summon James here, instead of meeting him on the street or in a pub. The other reason was, of course, to ensure that James understood it was a professional meeting, not a chance for him to try to reconcile with her.

"Well, you've got plenty of chassis here," she said. "Hook it up. I'll disconnect it after it puts you into a stupor."

"You two work in the closet while I get my men back to work," Reynolds said.

Susan and James went into the back room, where James had backup systems for Planetary Warning and the overseas radio links. Then he set the alien device on a counter, hung his jacket over a chair, and set to work. "You moved to the city," he said.

"Yep," Susan said.

"You always wanted to live there."

"Yeah. I guess I did."

James plugged in a soldering iron, then disconnected a chassis and lifted it out of a spare radio frame.

"When does the national network go live?" Susan asked, steering the topic to less personal—and more relevant—ground.

"It was going to be for Thanksgiving weekend, but they moved it up to October thirtieth yesterday," James said, examining the connections on the alien chassis before fashioning a cable for it.

"But that's in two days! How will they distribute the radios that fast? And how the hell are they building them so quickly?"

"Language, Susan. Have you been hanging out with sailors?"

"Veterans, actually."

"I don't know how GE turned out the radios so fast, but they've distributed more than half a million now. It's unbelievable. Abrams and I were talking about it yesterday. It's like they opened a new manufacturing facility or something."

A new facility? "Like in Kearny?" Susan asked.

"Kearny?" James said. "Isn't that a town right over the Hudson in New Jersey?"

"Yes. We think there's . . . something going on over there." Susan wasn't sure if she wanted to explain the disappearances to James.

"I haven't heard anything about it," he said as he inspected the cable.

"Lieutenant Boggs mentioned it once."

"Is he one of your veterans?" James asked as he stood and started fitting the cable.

"No, he's the general's new driver. You've never spoken to him?"

"Hold on. I'm ready to try this. I'm guessing on the input voltages, but this alien stuff looks pretty tough. Here we go." James toggled on the device's power. "No smoke. Now I'll turn up the gai—"

The familiar droning sound from the device started, cutting James off. He stumbled back into the chair he'd used when fashioning the cable.

Susan counted to thirty, then turned the device off. James blinked, but he remained stock-still long enough to make her worry. Then he shook his head and surveyed the room. "What happened?" he asked.

"Do you believe me now?" Susan asked.

"What happened?" he repeated, holding his hands to his temples.

"You turned up the gain."

The door to the closet swung open, nearly hitting Susan. "What the hell was that?" Reynolds roared.

"You felt it, too?" James asked.

"That was it?" Reynolds asked, his eyes open wide. "You turned it on?"

Susan nodded.

"It's real," James said.

"Yeah," Reynolds replied as he closed the door behind him. "And we need to figure something out."

"The network goes live in two days," Susan told him.

Reynolds gaped. "Why doesn't that thing work on you? Are women immune?"

"Yes, Captain, it's our alien biology."

"Really?"

Susan groaned. "No. I saw women affected by it at that church."

"Didn't you have hearing troubles after the explosion at Edison?" James asked.

That was it! Whatever frequencies this device attacked must have been damaged in Susan's hearing. She nodded. "That must be it," she said.

"You need to stop it, Brogan," Reynolds said. "Sabotage the transmitter. Whatever it takes."

"The transmitter is already up and running," James said. "They've been sending out test broadcasts to newspapers, a few public places, and so forth."

"I've heard," Susan added. "We have one at *The Spectator*. Round the clock propaganda."

"*The Spectator*?" James asked. "You're working there?"

Susan nodded.

"With Urich? Are you two . . ."

"My God, James, he's almost old enough to be my dad," Susan snapped. "And women can go for entire weeks without boyfriends, you know."

James turned his eyes away like a scolded puppy.

"If you two are done, we need to come up with a plan here," Reynolds said.

"Well, I have the beginnings of one," Susan said. "But before I do that, let me tell you both how we found this device, and what our old friend Sean Fleming is up to."

CHAPTER 26

"So you're not going with your initial plan?" Carl asked.

"No," Susan said. "James pointed out that we don't know whether Fleming—or whoever he's working for—is going to connect those devices to the main transmitter, or override it like they did last time. And we can't sit there and override the broadcast forever. At some point, they'll find our transmitter and disable it. So we destroy the transmitters *and* the radios."

"Destroy them?" Sam said.

Susan sipped her coffee and placed it back on the morgue counter, taking extra care not to spill any on the tax records she had assembled for the city editor. "We received plans from Europe for a device based on the radioactive power supplies found in the Martian Tripods. When triggered, it disables all electronic devices within its immediate area."

"You're talking about the radioflash weapon those soldiers used in Reims?" Carl asked.

"Yes," Susan said.

"The one that exploded and took out a square kilometer of ground?" Carl asked.

"Yes, that's the one," Susan said. "But the German soldiers

worked out how to build smaller ones. We have a pair of smaller units." The plan was insane, but what choice did she and the others have?

"So it's a bomb?" Sam asked, arching an eyebrow. "You're going to trigger a bomb?"

"Yes, but that's only a side effect," Susan said.

"Oh, well then, that's fine," Sam said dismissively. "Just as long as the destruction is incidental."

"Better than having a big chunk of the city's populace frozen by that mind control device," Susan said. "James built two smaller radioflashes from a single Martian power unit earlier this year. But before he could test them, he was redirected to the National Radio Network. Now the radioflashes are sitting in a warehouse in West Orange. Nobody will miss them, at least not until they figure out what happened."

"So you have two completely untested explosive weapons built from plans transmitted over the radio," Carl said with a grin. "Sounds perfect."

"Where do you lunatics plan on setting these things up?" Sam asked.

"Thing," Susan corrected him. "We're holding one back in case they have their own transmitter set up somewhere else. Reynolds will be listening from Sayville, with at least one man wearing hearing protection, to make sure we knock them out. The radioflash will be at the Tesla site. It's already damaged and contaminated from the fire, and within the range of the national transmitter at the Metropolitan Life Building."

"They put it there?" Carl asked. "That's interesting."

"Nothing sinister there," Susan said. "It's the tallest building and has more than adequate power. James selected it."

"So when are they moving the weapons in?" Sam asked.

"I'm meeting Captain Reynolds and a few of his men tonight," Susan said, bracing herself for Sam's reaction. "James arranged for them to pick up the units in West Orange."

"You are?" Sam grumbled.

"Yes, I am. James needs to be at Edison early tomorrow, and he can't look like he spent the night in no-man's-land in New York City. I'm going to help the men set up the wireless detonator. I've seen it before, and making a mistake with it would be disastrous."

"Why not put a timer on it and set it off tonight?" Carl suggested. "It would destroy the transmitters and all the receivers."

"We want to make sure we disable their device, too," Susan answered. "We don't know whether it's in the city yet."

"Sounds like a plan," Carl said. "But you realize this is an attack on the United States government, right? That's a step up from working for a newspaper that William Jennings Bryan doesn't like."

Susan shrugged. "Someone's got to act. You told me to stand up for the truth. And the truth is, someone is threatening everyone in this city, and since they seem to at least have help from the government, we have no one to turn to."

"Well, you're not going there alone tonight," Sam said.

"I'm going to be escorted by a platoon of marines," Susan said with a grin.

"Marines?" Sam exclaimed. "Heaven help you, you need an army man."

"I don't know if we have enough radiation suits," Susan said.

"I survived Little Bighorn," Sam scoffed. "I'm not afraid of invisible radio waves."

CHAPTER 27

"This entrance is just sitting here unguarded?" Susan asked. "I thought we'd have to sneak in somehow."

"They left this passage in the wall for carting out contaminated material," Captain Reynolds said as Hornburger, one of his marines, closed the gate behind them. "The New York City Police guarded it for a few years, then threw a chain on it and left."

"Based on the map I dug up, there's a good spot over here," Susan said, pointing to her right. She'd located what should be a brownstone far enough from the perimeter that it wouldn't damage any occupied buildings on the other side, but still away from the most contaminated areas.

They reached a side street lined with residential units. Susan gestured to an alley. "You can park there," she told Hornburger. The marine was tall and lanky, but his exposed arms were thick with the muscle of a steelworker or mason.

"You're worried about the truck being out of sight?" Reynolds asked.

"You said no one guards this place anymore. Why take any risks?"

Reynolds shrugged. They all exited the truck and headed around to the back of the vehicle.

"About damn time," Sam muttered as he climbed out of the back of the truck. "I spent the whole ride waiting for this thing to go off!"

"I told you, sir, Brogan said it's perfectly stable without the triggering unit," said McConaghey, a giant of a man. He bit off the end of a cigar and lit it.

"Don't call me 'sir,'" Sam growled. "I worked for a living."

"Army?" Reynolds asked.

"Seventh Cavalry. Retired in '94."

Reynolds tilted his head to one side. "So you enlisted in '74? With the Seventh?"

"Yes. And before you ask, I was in Benteen's battalion."

Reynolds nodded and turned to Susan. "Where are we going?"

"First floor of any one of these places will do," Susan said. "We can work with some cover inside."

Sam and the marines got to work, hauling the steel barrel off the back of the truck and up the shallow stairs to the first floor and into the front door of the closest home. They stood the unit up in a sitting room that must have been elegant and well-loved a decade ago. Its high plaster ceiling still echoed with the comings and goings of a loving family, but it was cloaked with a veil of dust and cobwebs that shone in the moonlight filtering through cracked, grime-streaked windows. A mahogany piano, its ivory keys yellowed, rested beside a towering bookshelf whose spines—tattered volumes of Dickens, Whitman, and illustrated children's tales—asked to be read again.

As Susan crouched down and extended a hand to McConaghey for the wireless fuse, her eye caught a small porcelain doll in the corner. Her delicate face was cracked and her painted dress was frayed, a mute witness to the panic that must have forced her family to flee so quickly that they'd forgotten her. Panic caused by Tesla's fire which was, in turn, a result of Sean Fleming selling Martian hardware on the black market.

Susan turned away from the doll and double-checked that the battery was disconnected from the fuse. Then she attached it to three canon plugs protruding from the top of the radioflash. "There we go," she said.

But before she could connect the battery, someone spoke outside. "Where the hell did that truck come from?" the voice asked.

"I smell cigars," said a familiar voice. "Whoever it is, they're still nearby. Fan out. Check these houses."

Reynolds stared daggers at McConaghey, who shrugged sheepishly.

Reynolds pulled a pistol from his jacket, and the rest of the men followed his lead.

"It can't be," whispered Susan.

Reynolds cocked his head toward her.

"Fleming," she replied. Was it really him? Was he using this as a staging area for the kidnappings? Based on what Susan had read, most researchers thought the radiation was only a hazard with prolonged or repeated exposure. This was a terrible place to set up a headquarters. Maybe Fleming didn't know how contaminated the area was?

McConaghey, crouched down by the window, held up four fingers.

"We're evenly matched," Reynolds said.

"We don't want to talk to him?" Sam asked.

"He knows Susan, and he might recognize me," Reynolds said. "He won't talk."

"His loss," Sam grumbled.

"One of them is headed here," McConaghey said.

Reynolds gestured to Hornburger, who reholstered his weapon and positioned himself by the front door. It opened a moment later, and one of Fleming's leather-clad men took a few steps inside. A wiry forearm wrapped itself around his neck. The man struggled for a few tense moments before going limp.

"One down," whispered Reynolds.

Hornburger tied and gagged the man, then offered his weapon to Susan. She held up her hands and shook her head. Hornburger shrugged and put the extra gun in his belt.

"Anything in there, Yoder?" shouted Fleming from outside.

Minutes passed like slow summer hours. Eventually, Reynolds gestured to McConaghey, who silently crept toward the back of the house.

"Goddammit!" Fleming yelled, still outside the brownstone. "You, take the back. I've got the front. You cover me."

"We need to question him," Susan whispered. This was supposed to be an easy operation, but it had just gotten a lot more complicated. At least they might be able to learn something, though.

Reynolds nodded to Hornburger, who tipped his chin back in acknowledgment.

Fleming opened the door and took the same path his first man had. Hornburger grabbed him, but Fleming reacted quickly, stepping aside, twisting, and sending the marine to the floor. Then Fleming raised his gun and fired twice.

Reynolds roared as he hurled himself at Fleming, tackling him and sending both of them flying into the brownstone's front door. Glass splintered, but the door held. Fleming rebounded back and took a fist from Reynolds to his midsection, then his face.

Sam lunged for Fleming's weapon, which had fallen onto the parquet floor of the entrance foyer. When he picked it up, he tossed it to Susan. "Keep this out of reach," he said.

Susan caught Fleming's gun in two hands, surprised by how heavy it was. She stuffed it into one of her coat pockets.

A thumping noise rose from the back of the house, but it was impossible to see what was happening. Susan debated moving for a better vantage point when someone shouted from the street.

"What's going on in there?" It was Fleming's fourth man.

Fleming staggered to his feet with a knife in his right hand. He swung it wildly toward Reynolds, who stepped out of range.

"Get in here!" Fleming bellowed. He lunged toward Reynolds again, who dodged the end of the knife, then pushed Fleming back to the door.

"You've killed four of my men now," Reynolds said. "We'll settle this alone."

"I have no idea who you are," Fleming retorted.

A gun fired several shots from the street, sending a bullet through the hole left by the broken glass in the front door.

"Stop shooting, you idiot!" Fleming shouted.

Sam turned and ran toward the back door, nearly colliding with McConaghey. "With me!" Sam told him. "We need to stop that idiot outside."

After a few more shots, the shooting stopped. Susan dared a peek outside. Fleming's fourth man had taken cover behind an overgrown hedge. But after a few moments, his head popped out, and he opened fire again.

Someone inside the house groaned. Fleming fell to the ground, the knife clattering out of his hand. Reynolds kicked it away from him.

Susan and Reynolds reached Fleming at the same time. He was bleeding profusely from a leg wound. Susan fought the urge to gloat. He deserved it. But they still needed to talk to him. Reynolds took off his jacket and used Fleming's knife to cut a long strip of cloth for a tourniquet. Fleming winced in pain as the marine captain tightened the cloth around his leg.

"Hurts?" Reynolds said. "Good."

"What are you doing with those people?" Susan asked.

"Wouldn't you like to know?" Fleming said.

"That's your femoral artery," Reynolds added, nodding at the tourniquet. "I remove this, and you're dead in a couple of minutes."

"So you're a doctor now?" Fleming asked.

"No. A combat veteran." Reynolds tightened the tourniquet a bit more. "I can make sure you lose this leg, too. Honest mistake."

Fleming groaned. "We're manufacturing the radios over the river in some abandoned factory," he said. "We need the labor."

"And the mind control device?" Susan asked. "Is that for when the network goes live?"

"You know about—" Fleming started, then looked at Susan for a moment. "That was you, wasn't it? You slugged Filby. God, you're a pain in the ass."

Susan snorted.

"Who's involved in this?" Reynolds asked. "The White House? Just the SPs? The military?"

"I'm sure you'd love to find out," Fleming said. He reached for his knife, and Reynolds twisted so that Fleming only caught him in the shoulder. The marine captain fell back with a shout. Fleming lunged again and grabbed Reynolds's gun.

Weeks later, when trying to describe the moment to Jill, Susan still couldn't remember how she'd gotten the gun out of her coat so quickly. Nor could she believe that it had been cocked and ready to fire the entire time she'd been carrying it.

She fired a single shot that hit Fleming in the chest.

Sean Fleming's eyes flared. He coughed up blood, then moaned as he slumped to the floor. The last thing he said before he died was, "Such a pain in the ass. . . ."

CHAPTER 28

"You're sure that's going to work from all the way up here?" asked Sam as Susan sat with him and Carl in Jasper's office at *The Spectator*. "If they trigger that signal, you won't want to take a subway, and that battery is too heavy to carry."

"The troops used these wireless detonators in Mexico," Susan said. "They have five miles of range in an urban setting." She checked the connection from the lead-acid battery to the trigger for what seemed like the tenth time in five minutes. Despite Fleming's best efforts, the radioflash device was ready in no-man's-land, and she needed to stop playing with the detonator before she broke something.

"You sound like a sales brochure," Carl said.

"Well, I helped write the proposals for the War Department."

Carl grinned, then glanced at Jasper's wall clock. "Fifteen minutes."

The three of them had moved the radio back to Jasper's office and switched it on. Now, the volume was turned low enough that the static made for a strangely comforting background noise. Susan raised her cup of coffee to her lips. She shouldn't be drinking coffee this late in the day, but it wasn't like she was going to get any sleep. She might never sleep again.

"It's not going to go away," Sam said.

"Huh?" asked Susan.

"The image."

"I'm not thinking about that."

"Really? So how did you know what I was talking about?"

Susan looked away.

"I killed my first man on June twenty-fifth, 1876," Sam went on. "We were pinned down on a bluff for hours until night fell. Captain Benteen led a counterattack at one point, and my platoon was recruited. Those natives were tough. We were pinned down, yeah, but we had the high ground. They were shooting at rocks, and we were shooting at them. But then they got smart and hunkered down in the high grass and started crawling up on us. Would have been a bloodbath if Benteen hadn't taken us out there and pushed them back."

"I thought Little Bighorn *was* a bloodbath," Susan said.

"Oh, it was, over in Custer's valley. But it could have been a hell of a lot worse. Anyway, I got separated from the group in the tall grass and blundered right into one of the natives." Sam's voice thickened as he added, "Couldn't have been a day older than I was. He was faster than me. Reached out and slapped my rifle right out of my hands and bore down on me with his hatchet. I still have the reminder right here." He pointed at his right shoulder with his left hand.

"We wrestled. I was bigger than him, but he was strong. Wiry. Nearly impossible to get a hold of. So at some point, I got my knife out and . . . that was it." He stopped and stared ahead. "I'll never lose that image. I just learned to live with it."

"You had to defend yourself," Carl said. "Just like Susan did."

Susan took another sip of coffee. "Thank you, Sam," she said.

"Welcome to the National Radio Network, where we bring you all the news you need to know," said the radio.

"Either that clock is slow, or his is fast," said Carl.

Susan sat up straight in her chair.

"This is Johnny Tarlek. Today in Washington, President Bryan signed the National Identification Act into law. This law will require all United States citizens to carry and show legally recognized identification on demand from any authorized Security Police or military officer as of January first, 1917. This gives states two years to issue identification to their citizens. This law will make the streets safer and . . ."

"Well, I saw that one coming," Carl said.

The broadcast continued, with Susan on the edge of her chair for the next twenty minutes. The droning never happened. Sam and Carl debated the merits of the identification law. Jasper came and went from his office.

Susan sat back in her seat with a sigh. Had stopping Sean Fleming ended the conspiracy? The government must have known how the radios were being manufactured. But had they been working with the Martians on the mind control device?

"Ladies and gentlemen, it seems funny to say during our first broadcast, but this is most irregular," Johnny Tarlek said, and Susan's attention snapped back to the radio. "I have news that's happening even as I speak to you. We have reports of a Martian Tripod in Jersey City, New Jersey. I repeat, a Martian has been spotted in New Jersey. And we have a report of more Tripods joining it, and now"—he paused for a few moments—"at least one in New York City."

Susan's heart leaped into her throat. The Martians were here —and on the attack. Had she caused this when she'd killed Fleming? Or was this their plan all along?

"Now I have word that the sailors and soldiers at Fort Columbus have been mobilized," Johnny Tarlek continued. "The secretary of war and National Security Secretary Comstock are asking everyone who can hear this broadcast to stay in their homes until further notice." An edge of fear had crept into his voice by then.

Sam rose and peered out the window. "Good luck with that. People are already headed to all the river crossings."

Had the plan been to trigger the device and then attack? Was the idea to make people easier to capture? Or to paralyze the military, who would likely be required to listen to the broadcast?

"Susan," Carl said.

Susan jumped at the sound of her name. "Yes?"

"Trigger it," said Carl.

"What?"

"The radioflash device. The Germans invented it to stop Martians. Stop the Martians."

Of course. Susan had been waiting for one particular cue when a better one had now presented itself.

She rose, walked to the trigger sitting next to the radio, and pressed the button. Nothing happened.

She pressed the button again. Still nothing.

She jiggled the power connection, played with the small aerial, and even disconnected the battery and crossed the wires to check for a charge. Eventually, she was rewarded with a spark. So the battery had a charge, but the trigger wasn't working.

"Well?" Sam asked.

"Maybe we do need to take it outside," Susan suggested. "The walls might be blocking the signal. Someone take the battery. I'll carry the trigger."

Sam scooped up the battery as Susan ran with the device. They hit the elevator at a run, and Carl pushed the button for the ground floor. He fussed with his jacket while Sam stoically hoisted the battery in both hands.

The elevator stopped. As the door started to open, an explosion echoed in the distance. The lights went out, and the elevator door stopped. Susan suppressed a yelp of surprise.

"What was that?" Carl asked.

"Martians must've hit a power line or the station itself," Sam said.

One of the men struck a match. The door was less than a third of the way open. Sam braced a hand on each side and strained to pull them further away from each other. "It's stuck," he said. "You'll fit through, Susan. Go try to find something to pry it open."

Susan turned to one side and squeezed through the opening, holding the trigger under one arm. She was afraid of putting it down and having it be lost or crushed underfoot.

"Who's there?" asked a deep voice.

"Louie!" bellowed Sam from inside the elevator. "It's Dodds! The damn elevator's stuck. Get over here!"

Thunderous footfalls sounded from behind Susan before the paper's regular security guard barreled into her, knocking her to the floor—and launching the trigger out of her arms.

"No!" Susan said.

"Sorry," Louie mumbled.

Susan scrambled in the dark, struggling to use cautious, probing fingers and the meager ambient light to find the trigger. The sound of a steel door sliding open made her jump as her fingers brushed something.

"Wait!" she shouted.

"What?" Sam asked.

"Don't move," Susan said. "I dropped it."

"What are you talking about?" asked Carl.

"I dropped the detonator when Louie bumped into me. It's somewhere on the floor."

"Said I was sorry," Louie said.

Before anyone else could respond, an earsplitting howl sounded from outside. The howl of a Martian Tripod.

Susan gasped. The noise transported back to her hiding place under a desk at elementary school in Ridgewood. This was the machine that had nearly leveled her hometown and had killed both her parents. She held her head in her hands, relieved that the men couldn't see her panicking.

"What the hell was that?" asked Louie.

"Lived all your life in the city, Louie?" Carl asked.

"Yeah. Why?"

"It was a Martian. They're here."

"What are we gonna do?"

"Got a lantern, Louie?" asked Sam.

"What?"

"A lantern," Carl said. "So we can see."

"Oh. Yeah, lemme go get it."

"Wait!" Susan said, praying Louie missed the detonator as he thundered by.

Light spilled into the entrance foyer, forcing Susan to blink as she wiped away a tear before anyone could see. She spotted the trigger then and grabbed it. When she approached the lamp and inspected the device under the light, she found it was—mercifully—intact.

"Let's go," she said, and walked out onto 52nd Street . . . and into sheer chaos.

The street was flooded with people pushing and shoving to head west. A howl drew Susan's attention and showed her why: a Martian Tripod was lumbering toward her from the east.

People pushed past Susan, forcing her between a parked truck and the building's cold brick wall. She clutched the trigger to her chest with both arms and held on. Where was Sam? He could plow through this crowd and make a path for her so that a clear—or at least a clearer—line of sight to where the radioflash was in no-man's-land. He had the battery, too.

The Tripod howled again, then strode north and out of sight. After a few more minutes, the crowd thinned out.

"There you are," said Sam, appearing from behind the truck. His hands were empty.

"Where's the battery?" Susan asked.

"In there," he said, pointing one thumb toward the truck. "You said we weren't close enough. Let's drive a few blocks south?" It was a sad-looking bread truck, with worn, steel-rimmed wooden wheels, a hole in one side, and only two seats in the front.

"Where's Carl?" Susan asked.

"Back here, holding the battery," said Carl from the back of the truck.

Susan climbed into the front seat. Sam jogged to the front and looked down at the front of the truck before he threw up his hands. Susan reached over to the starter button and pushed it. The truck sprang to life. Sam grinned, jumped behind the wheel, and threw the truck into gear with a grind of metal against metal.

The truck hurdled down 52nd, narrowly missing a man carrying a child, and turned onto Park Avenue. Sam shifted his position in the driver's seat, forcing Susan to shift her weight as she clutched the detonator.

Less than four blocks later, Sam was forced to slam on the brakes. An overturned carriage was blocking 48th Street.

"Shit," he muttered, and turned east. The truck cut south on 3rd Avenue, skidding before Sam drove it at speed for more than ten blocks.

"Is this close enough?" he bellowed over the protests of the truck's engine.

"I think s—"

Susan was cut off by a gut-wrenching hum as a heat ray cut the air in front of the truck. Sam slammed on the brakes. The truck skidded, struck something in the road, and the world spun before everything went black..

For a moment, there was nothing. Consciousness returned to Susan with the howl of a Martian Tripod and a sharp pain in her right ankle. She was lying on the street, thrown out of the truck.

The Tripod loomed over 3rd Avenue. Susan started to scramble away, but the pain in her ankle forced her to stop. It was broken.

The heat ray, trained on something out of view, hummed to life again.

And then Susan remembered. The detonator! Turning, she discovered the truck on its side about twenty feet away.

Susan pulled herself along the sidewalk with her hands and pushed with her left leg, trying not to scream with each move and attract attention from the nearby Martian. After minutes that passed like hours, she reached the truck. But how was she going to get over its side and then inside to find the detonator? Maybe through the windscreen?

She slid herself around to the truck's front and cut her hand on glass shards on the ground. Yes! That meant the windscreen had shattered. After a few more agonizing minutes, she located the device on the street, about twenty feet from the wreck. If she survived, she'd have to tell James that it was ready for field duty. It wasn't so much as scratched.

Now, the battery.

"Susan."

She glanced up to find Carl. He was standing over her, holding a broken piece of metal in one hand and his side with the other.

"It's broken," he said.

Susan's heart sank. They were doomed. She should have stayed at *Spectator* headquarters. She would have been killed, but this? This madness could have been stopped. Maybe she shouldn't have panicked and killed Fleming. If she hadn't, maybe this attack wouldn't have begun.

"Doesn't the damn truck have one of those?" Sam asked. He was leaning against the overturned truck. His face was streaked with blood and he seemed to be holding one arm at a strange angle.

He was right. This was a military device, designed to work off the army's truck batteries if need be.

Carl was already at the truck's hood and awkwardly opening it. The truck's battery was secured on the vehicle's right side, which was up in the air. "What now?" he asked.

The heat ray throbbed again, striking a building across Third Avenue.

"Give me a knife," said Susan, "and those wires from the broken battery." She took a blade from Sam and skinned the wires. "Red on positive, black on negative," she told Carl.

Carl's brow furrowed.

"The truck should have the same colors," Susan clarified.

He nodded, turned, and connected the wires.

"Now twist the other ends on these, and push the button," Susan said. "I can't stand."

Carl connected the black wire and drew a spark when he connected the red one. He flinched.

"That's fine!" Susan shouted. "Push the button!"

Carl pressed the button.

Seconds later, a deafening explosion sounded from downtown. The cloud of smoke and debris was still rising when Susan opened her eyes and looked to the south. Then her attention was drawn by a creaking sound behind her.

The Tripod tipped to one side, then the other, and finally fell in her direction, missing Susan, Carl, and Sam by five very short feet.

CHAPTER 29

"This is your office?" said Jill as she paced back and forth in front of Susan's counter, spinning so she could take in the entire morgue.

"I don't know if I'd call it 'mine,' or an office, but it's where I spend my days," Susan said, hobbling over to a chair and fumbling with her crutches.

"Wow," said Jill. "This must be amazing. I think I'd lose my mind in here, but it's perfect for a bookworm like you." She must have noticed that Susan was struggling, because she rushed over to grab the crutches.

Susan laughed. "Excuse me? Bookworm?"

"I'm sorry. I meant 'well-read intellectual.'"

"Thank you," said Susan, then nodded at the crutches. "And thank you for that, too. Just a few more weeks with those cursed things."

"The price of being a heroine," Jill said, snickering.

"An anonymous heroine," Susan whispered. No one could ever know what she, Carl, and Sam had done during the Martian attack a few weeks earlier. They'd stopped an alien invasion of New York City, but to do it, they'd detonated a bomb. By doing so, as Carl had pointed out later, they'd also attacked the United

States government by destroying part of the National Radio Network, which prevented the government from spreading more disinformation. That would never be an effective defense in court, though, if Susan and the others were ever caught.

Unsurprisingly, the Security Police and the military were not pleased about this. They were now looking for the perpetrators, but any evidence had gone up in a literal cloud of smoke. A "mushroom cloud," according to the *Post*. So far, no one had noticed the missing Martian power supplies from Edison's warehouse. James had assured Susan that this would continue to be the case, since the inventories had been a mess going back to when Sean Fleming had pillaged them for profit.

"And not a good enough heroine to save more of the prisoners at Kearny Point," Susan continued, speaking louder now.

"But they're free now, aren't they?" Jill asked. "And didn't they find your old boss there?"

"Yes, Ben Johnson was there," Susan answered. Kearny Point had been left in ruins when police from Jersey City had arrived there after the attack. More than 3,000 people had been forced into labor there, manufacturing radios for the national network under the supervision of another prisoner: Ben Johnson. James had sent a car from Edison with the news, and an offer to drive her to visit him in the hospital.

"He's recovering over in New Jersey," Susan said, her breath catching in her throat as she thought of their tearful reunion the week before. "He's going to be okay, and it looks he'll be taking over the radio team when he's up to it."

The Jersey City police—and members of the local press—had arrived at Kearny Point before the federal government, so the word about what had happened there went out before they could stop it.

The Jersey Journal had run the story the next morning; and according to Jasper, when the SPs had shown up at the publisher's office, he'd shown them what he'd decided not to publish: that there had been no Martian damage west of Kearny Point. In other words, it seemed like the Martians had started their rampage at Kearny. The SPs had left the publisher with a sternly worded threat, and the publisher had left for an extended trip to Europe a few days after talking to Jasper.

"Just another day in the trenches," Jasper had said.

"But they're free, and that girl you were looking for came home, right?" Jill asked.

"Yeah, Lisa made it home," Susan said wistfully.

"Are you sure you're not thinking about going back?" Jill asked with a raised eyebrow. "Old habits are hard to break,"

"Absolutely not," Susan said.

She had thought about it, but Jill didn't need to know that. General Ross had been carted out of his office at Edison in hand-cuffs and James had wasted no time announcing that he was stepping down to let Ben Johnson take over his old spot. So things could largely return to how they had been last year. But there was no going back for Susan. She couldn't trust James again, and she couldn't go back to babysitting radio engineers and whoever the next War Department liaison would be. She had moved on.

The elevator door opened then, and Jasper Bell walked out. "Susan! You're here," he said as he approached with a mug in one hand and a plate in the other. "Welcome back! I thought you might have problems carrying your morning coffee and break-fast with those damned crutches. I hated them when I turned my ankle playing tennis." He turned toward Jill then. "Oh! Hello! And who is this?"

"Good morning, Jasper," Susan said. "You really shouldn't have. And this is Jill. She's helping me out on my first day back."

"That's very kind of her," Jasper said as he extended a hand toward Jill and regaled her with that smile. "I hope to see you around again, Jill. Well, off to a meeting. Maybe I'll check in with you later." He stepped back toward the elevator, then stopped. "Oh, and Susan?" he asked.

"Yes?"

"When you're up to it, feel free to talk to the city editor about an assignment," he said with a smile, then disappeared.

An assignment? A lump formed in Susan's throat. That had been Jasper's way of telling her Susan was a reporter now. *The Spectator* had to pass on the story, but that didn't mean he wasn't going to reward Susan for her work. She considered hobbling over to the elevator and taking it down to the city desk before Jasper changed his mind. But no, she didn't have to. She had earned this.

"Is he married?" Jill asked.

"Yes," Susan said.

"Liar."

"I don't need my best friend to be dating my boss," Susan said. "Not to mention long-distance relationships never work."

"What distance? Your apartment building has a vacancy, and you're going to be too busy chasing stories for dating."

Susan looked at her friend and smiled. "I hope you're not asking me for a reference, Jill, I don't know if that building can handle one more troublesome young lady."

ABOUT THE AUTHOR

I'm Eric Goebelbecker. I write stuff.

I'm the author of *Shadows of the Past, Clouds in the Future,* and *Murder in Soft Words,* the first three books in an ongoing series about the aftermath of the Martin invasion in the War of the Worlds.

I was lucky enough to inherit an incurable curiosity about technology and a tremendous love of science fiction from his father. Both led to a career repairing radars in the U.S. Army, followed by another as a programmer on Wall Street. Now, I write about technology and train dogs, as well as work on my sci-fi and fantasy stories.

If you're not already a subscriber, you can find my email list here, get a free short story about Ben Johnson and get the latest news on my next book and short stories.

Find me at my newsletter, on my website, and on the social links below.

And please consider leaving a review!

facebook.com/egoebelbecker

instagram.com/egoebelbecker

bsky.app/profile/ericgoebelbecker.com